INTERSTELLAR PORTALS

COMPLETE SERIES

JINX LAYNE

NO REGERTS PRESS, LLC

Published by No Regerts Press, LLC

NO REGERTS
PRESS, LLC

Cover Designed by Kasmit Covers

ISBN 978-1-957933-13-9 (print)

Join my mailing list here:
www.jinxlayne.com

CONTENTS

WARRIOR MINE

Chapter 1   3
Leah

Chapter 2   6
Ax'ryon

Chapter 3   10
Leah

Chapter 4   13
Ax'ryon

Chapter 5   16
Leah

Chapter 6   23
Ax'ryon

Chapter 7   26
Leah

Chapter 8   33
Ax'ryon

Chapter 9   36
Leah

Chapter 10   43
Ax'ryon

Chapter 11   45
Leah

Chapter 12   52
Ax'ryon

KRAKEN MINE

Chapter 1   61
Kaia

Chapter 2   64
Ty'zir

Chapter 3   69
Kaia

Chapter 4   73
Ty'zir

Chapter 5   78
Kaia

Chapter 6   81
Ty'zir

Chapter 7   88
Kaia

Chapter 8   96
Ty'zir

Chapter 9   101
Kaia

Chapter 10   105
Ty'zir

Chapter 11   108
Kaia

REBEL MINE

Chapter 1   115
Shawna

Chapter 2   120
Gar'ek

Chapter 3   123
Shawna

Chapter 4   129
Gar'ek

Chapter 5   133
Shawna

Chapter 6   140
Gar'ek

Chapter 7   146
Shawna

Chapter 8   154
Gar'ek

Epilogue   158

About the Author   161

WARRIOR MINE

INTERSTELLAR PORTALS BOOK 1

JINX LAYNE

1

LEAH

"Don't look back, just keep moving forward!" Our guide, Stream (yes...*Stream*...I know, I know), shouted encouragements at us through the pouring rain as I gripped the side of the mountain for dear life. "Let the healing rain wash away your negative self-talk and misconceptions. You can do anything!"

I pictured him writing all of this in his hemp-covered meditation journal, thinking he'd hit profound paydirt, then packing up the artisanal cheese he'd made in his roommate's pottery-studio-slash-potato-pantry and biking over to the farmers' market to barter.

Too much? Maybe. I tend to get snarky when staring death in the face. The trail before me was quickly disintegrating, now more mud than anything else. Still, I took Stream's clichéd advice, bravely stepped forward—

And slid! *Shit!*

I pushed my back flat against the wall of wet dirt and tangled roots, struggling to regain my footing.

What the hell was I doing here, again? *Finding myself?* That's what my friends had told me I should do after my fiancé,

Darren, dumped me for his new secretary—sorry, "executive assistant".

"Go on one of those adventure hikes in Kaua`i and figure out who you want to be!" Shawna, my fitness-obsessed friend, had suggested with a wild look in her eyes. "The Kalalau Trail is *amaaaazing*!"

Funny, with how excited she seemed, not to mention how supportive my other friends were about this ridiculous idea, every single one of them had found some excuse why they couldn't join me.

Were they really too busy? Or was it that they weren't interested in risking their lives with their basket case of a friend?

Either way, I guess I didn't blame them, but as the wind picked up and slapped my hair across my face, I wondered why I couldn't just have been pampered for five days in the hotel spa.

Did my friends not know me at all?

Darren had claimed he didn't know me, either.

"You're not who I thought you were, babe," he'd told me with a sigh after I'd spent yet another long day at the office. "You're holding me back from my true potential." He'd wanted me to quit my job once we were married, but I liked working and earning my own money. I wasn't about to give up my independence to help him become head asshole—sorry, "CEO". But he'd assumed I'd be on board with being a trophy wife, so no, he really didn't know me. When his perky assistant with the even perkier tits, Jenna, made it clear she was more than happy to live that life, he sealed the deal with his dick, and I was history.

Ugh. He was the *last* person I should be thinking about right now.

The rain pelted me as I prepared to take another step. I glanced around, but no one was nearby. I must've fallen behind the group.

I stepped, but my foot never found solid ground. My boot merely grazed the muddy gravel, and I started to slide.

"No!" I scrambled to find purchase on the slippery rocks with any available limb.

My hands latched onto a handlebar-sized root, and I stopped sliding momentarily, dangling there as I felt about with my toes to find something stable and firm.

"Help!" I screamed. Nothing. All I could see above me was mountain, brush, and rock, blurred by the rain in my eyes.

If anyone replied, the wind swallowed their voices.

I yelled again, hoping someone would hear, or notice I was gone.

Then the root I held onto suddenly jerked. I yelled again. Was someone above trying to rescue me? Or was the root giving—

Snap!

I screamed as I fell straight down, cursing Stream, my friends, and my douchebag ex as I went.

2

AX'RYON

THE SKY WATER was loud and thick on the coast this day during my twenty-fifth star cycle alive. I glanced up to thank the gods for it. Sky water meant good things to come. Bounty. Abundance. Fortune.

The wet sand crunched under my webbed toes as I made my way around Elder Rock toward the Cave of Unmei. It was tradition in the clans of the Rex'ulti for a warrior to visit the cave when they reached adulthood. The cave would show the warrior their destiny, and then they were obliged to follow the path of truth to fulfill it.

I'd been waiting for this day since I was a child carrying a wooden spear, hoping the cave would show me leading my people against any enemy that dared threaten us. I'd been preparing and training for it all my life, making whatever sacrifices were necessary. It was all I'd ever wanted.

My ultimate dream.

The waves crashed along the shore, and my fins ached for water, longing for a swim. They'd been flexing all morning from excitement; I was so anxious. My mother had forced me to take a breakfast of miko berries and gahbi fruit when I'd stopped to see her on my way out.

"Your father would have wanted you to have a full belly when you received your destiny," she had said, shoving the food into my hands. "Go. Make him proud, my son."

My father had died in battle long ago against the Sun'ozi. An honorable death, but I missed him. He'd had wisdom and strength, and had always known exactly what to say to make me laugh and ease my over-stimulated nerves. It gave me pleasure to think that I was following my father's path as a warrior and, hopefully, a leader.

The entrance to the cave lay up ahead, the waves so high and rough they nearly obscured the mouth of it. As the tide pulled away from the shore, I saw that something was lying on the sand.

A body.

I sprinted toward the strange creature, skidding to a stop next to it and dropping to my knees.

A tiny female.

My chest pounded in my ears until I thought my heart might explode.

My mate.

I knew it the instant I touched her, caressing the delicate column of her neck with my large hand. A strange fire blazed through me and I shook with need, the connection between us awakening something deep, ancient, and...bestial. Gods, her sweet scent mixed with the salt of the ocean nearly drove me out of my mind.

Focus, Ax'ryon.

She was unconscious, but thank the gods still breathing. Her faint heartbeat pulsed under my fingers like a throbbing electric melody. I gathered her limp form in my arms, so small and fragile, and hurried into the cave to get her out of the storm

7

and away from the waves. There, I laid her out on a large, flat rock while I searched for evoki plants. Their balm would heal the wounds on her knees and arms.

The Cave of Unmei was exactly how my father had described it—spacious, with a glowing pool in the center, rock formations lining the walls and floor, and a vast array of dark fauna. The evoki plants were luminescent, making them easy to find amid the rock piles.

I returned to my mate. *Mate*. Just the word excited me.

Everything that the word evoked—bonding in mind, body, and soul—had not meant anything to me until that moment I saw her there on the sand. With my destiny as head of our clan always at the forefront of my mind, I had never stopped to think about what my future might include, aside from battle and celebration.

My mate was...odd. Definitely not Rex'ulti. She had no fins, gills, or scales. Nor was she Kisq'ali; there weren't any tentacles as far as I could see. Not even Sun'ozi, since she lacked creeping vines or leafy appendages. These were the only clans that currently lived on the planet Co'sentyx.

So what was she?

She had golden hair that fell in short waves from her head, a small nose, and a tiny flower bud mouth with lush lips that I ached to taste. I wished her eyes would open so I could see what glorious color they were. Her skin was tan and smooth, reminding me of the hide of a burak underneath all the fur. Intricate designs marked her skin in various spots on her upper arms, the colors pleasing and rich.

She wore strange blue material around her hips and upper thighs, and a small armless top clung to the curves of her torso, her breasts encased in some other garment. I groaned. It was exquisite torture to run my hands over her body as I felt for broken bones, and when I came to her groin, she made a desperate sound that made my cock throb.

Gods help me.

I tried to put that thought out of my mind as I used the evoki plant balm on her torn skin.

She began to shiver, and I crawled onto the rock to curl my body around hers. I removed her soaked upper and lower garments as best I could without inadvertently tearing them with my claws. I left the flimsy material covering her breasts and the scrap of fabric over her pelvis in place. I needed *something* between her body and mine. My loin pouch was already strained to its limits.

As we lay there together, her shivering stopped, and she even snuggled into me.

I smiled as her breathing got deeper. She slept.

Soon, I succumbed to sleep alongside her.

3

LEAH

I awoke with a gasp. I went to sit up, but found I was trapped under something heavy.

Okay, just stay calm. You're alive.

I stared out into the space in front of me, trying to get my bearings. I appeared to be in some sort of dark cave, with strange things glowing a wild neon nearby. Party lights, maybe? Shadows of undulating water and blue color reflected on the piles of rock and walls nearby. And it smelled...fishy.

Where was I? And why didn't I feel any pain? I'd fallen off a mountain that plunged straight into the sea, for God's sake!

Oh no. Could I be paralyzed?

I wiggled my fingers and toes experimentally. Everything was still moving as it was supposed to, thank God.

Then something shifted behind me, and I froze.

Whatever was boxing me in was alive, too!

Fuck.

"Morach najir yua e kenkali?" a deep, growling voice said from behind me. I nearly jumped out of my skin.

What the hell was that? A man?

I struggled in his grasp, trying to free myself and get away.

But his arms were massive and muscular, so thick and strong, and...

Oh God. Scaly.

What kind of fucked-up punked horror show was this?

"Let me go!" I screamed, pounding on him with every ounce of strength I had. I didn't survive that fall only to be manhandled by some cave-dwelling, roided-out gym rat with a gross skin condition.

He spoke more gibberish I didn't understand, initially tightening his grip. But as I fought and yelled, he gradually let go. I scrambled forward on my knees, got to my feet, wobbled, and nearly fell again. I reached for the nearest rock to hold me up.

"Najir, ackito!" he growled, his voice following me. I made it further into the cave and tripped. This time I turned onto my back and crab walked backward. I finally faced my captor.

And my jaw *dropped*.

The towering creature before me was almost twice the size of an average man in both height and width. His muscles were monstrous yet lean, and the markings on his skin reminded me of a koi fish...mottled and vibrant in gradients of neon orange and red against a glowing white background. Black rimmed his large yellow eyes. More black markings dotted his hands and feet, and fins. Yes, those were *fins* atop his head, which looked to continue down his back to his tail. *Tail?!* Did I mention he was naked? He was. Well, naked except for a leather-like loincloth slung around his hips and cradling his huge and erect—

"Morach najir," he whispered, his lips curling into a smile. It should've been creepy. But it wasn't.

What was I saying? This fish-guy-thing, whatever he was, hung out in dark caves, lying in wait for unsuspecting victims. Who cared if he was (sort of) handsome and (really) hung? He was about to tell me to put the lotion on my skin, I just knew it!

I got up to my feet as he watched, with an expression akin to concern.

Concern? Yeah, right. Stop reading stuff into this just because he's hot, Leah.

"Stay away from me, big guy," I said, using my most threatening voice. I glanced around the cave quickly and saw natural light off to the side. The entrance! Which would also be the exit!

I made a run for it before koi-man had a chance to react. Suddenly a loud rumble echoed around me, and pebbles, rocks, and dust began to rain down from above. I stopped to shield my face and head from the onslaught.

The cave was collapsing?! Christ, I couldn't catch a damn break.

I flung myself in the direction of the cave mouth as debris hailed down on me, but I could already tell the light was dimming. Shit!

My only chance to get out was making it to that light before it disappeared.

Koi-man yelled something from nearby.

I was getting close when a thundering crack stopped me in my tracks. I screamed and braced myself, expecting to be crushed to death by rocks.

No rocks. Instead a hard, warm body landed on top of me, and a thick, raspy voice whispered things that I didn't understand, but suddenly desperately wanted to. His voice slid over me, surrounding me as completely as his body did, a strange, but comforting sensation filling my very soul.

Um, wait. I was getting turned on by the monster voted most likely to eat me if we weren't killed by this rockslide first.

What the *hell* was my problem?

4

AX'RYON

I COVERED my mate with my body and my adrenaline surged, taking the weight of the falling rocks easily. I knew nothing of her species or from where she came, and she obviously didn't understand the language of Co'sentyx. The only thing I knew was that I needed to perform the bonding rite as soon as possible.

The cave had indeed shown me my destiny: it was this female. She was my mate. And now I was bound to protect her with my life.

The rocks above eventually slowed their descent, and despite the barrage of debris I was still able to move.

Praise the gods, we were both alive.

I raised up on all fours so as not to crush her, and her body trembled below me.

"You are safe, my mate," I murmured. She only whimpered.

I stood, brushed off the rubble, and looked up. The cave was still intact above us, but as I surveyed the rest of it, I saw the entrance was now completely blocked by rocks as large as me. The only light came from the luminescent foliage and the pool.

When I glanced back down at my mate, she was on her back staring up at me.

"Ohgodohgodohgodohgodohgod" she chanted, her eyes wide and terrified.

Why was she afraid? Hadn't she felt the bond's pull?

She entranced me like no other, her strange body calling to me despite her lacking any of the practical physical attributes of the clans on Co'sentyx. And her fresh scent was intoxicating. I longed to breathe her in and explore every part of her. Having my body wrapped around hers just now had been like reaching Tingokku, the pleasure such that my loin pouch once again gave away my arousal.

I squatted down, realizing she might be afraid of my size. She squeaked and scrambled backward until her back hit the wall. "Whatdoyouwantwithme?"

I had no idea what she was saying, but I needed her to understand. I wanted to tell her she need not fear me. I was her mate. Sworn to love and protect her. Always.

"We need to perform the bonding rite immediately, my mate." I walked closer to her and reached down to pull her up, but she pressed her back to the wall with such force her knuckles turned white.

"Whatareyoudoing?" she chattered.

I had to make her see. I grabbed her by the arm, my body thrumming with delight.

"No!Stop!Whatthehell?Getawayfromme!"

She fought me off as I made her stand, then I slid my hand around the side of her neck, my fingers tangled in her hair, my thumb against her jaw. Her eyes, which I could see now were a dark abyss of glorious mossy green, closed for a moment and she leaned into me. There... she *did* feel destiny's pull. But when her eyes opened again, she bucked, trying to break free of my grasp.

"My mate, please, trust me," I coaxed, and the tension in her body eased again. I grabbed her opposite hand and had her cup my neck, her thumb on my face, mirroring my hold on her.

We were ready.

She struggled, but I held her firm.

I leaned in and touched my forehead to hers, willing her to see into my mind's heart. To realize that fate had called us together because we were destined to be joined as one.

It felt like nothing I'd ever experienced before. Pleasure to the point of pain, as my hand throbbed from the rapid pulse in her neck. The more her heart pumped, the more my legs quaked.

My mate moved in closer, holding onto me as the bond deepened and then solidified.

Yes, my mate... Feel me. Feel *us*.

I feel you...her mind's heart responded, and I moaned with joy.

5

LEAH

KOI-MAN FINALLY LET GO of me and moved away. My eyes fluttered open.

"Can you understand me now, my mate?" he asked, and I blinked harder.

What the ever-loving hell was going on? First, we were nearly crushed by rocks. Then this creature saved me, before drawing me into some crazy trance where I could feel him. Like literally feel him *inside* of me, everywhere. And it wasn't bad at all. In fact, it was...exhilarating.

And now he was speaking English? The words he spoke earlier were anything but.

I reached for a nearby rock to steady myself. "Yes, I can understand you, but how? When your mouth moves it's not forming English words." I really couldn't help staring at his mouth. Shit, I needed to get a grip.

"It's the bonding rite," he explained, sitting down cross-legged and giving me *way* too generous a view of that pouch—okay, more like a giant eggplant sack—at his groin.

I cleared my throat, the dust in the cave still settling. "Umm...bonding rite?"

"The joining of the body and mind's heart. It brings to light all that needs to be understood if those who perform it are mates."

"Whoa, there." I held my hands out in front of me. "Mates?"

"Yes. You are my mate."

"Uh, how about no? I just met you. Besides, I don't even know where I am, how I got here, or what you are."

He chuckled and a small smile lit up his (okay yeah handsome) features. "You can deny it all you want, my mate, but the fates don't lie. I came to the Cave of Unmei to find my destiny, and there you were." His electric yellow eyes focused on me. "The bonding rite confirms it."

I shook off the warm feelings attempting to take hold of me. "N-no... I fell down a mountain during a hiking tour and woke up...in your...ginormous arms. I should be terrified of you," I huffed.

"But you are not, are you?"

I narrowed my eyes at him but didn't answer. He was right: I wasn't afraid of him anymore. I didn't exactly know why. Logically, I could think of dozens of reasons why I should be. Damn, this was weird.

A chill swept over me, and I realized I was only in my bra and panties. "Wait, where are my clothes?" My cheeks heated and I tried to cover myself with my hands.

He didn't look embarrassed at all. "They were soaked when I found you out in front of the cave. I had to remove them to keep you from illness. I used my body heat to warm you." He stood. "I can see you are shivering. Come, I'll warm you again." He reached for me, but I backed away.

"I'll be okay." I sat on a rock and grimaced. It was both cold and wet.

His gaze held mine, and his expression told me he was

fighting some kind of internal battle. "I'll build a fire for you, my mate."

"Stop calling me that."

Disappointment creased his forehead and mouth. "Then what should I call you?"

"My name is Leah."

"Lee'yah," he replied carefully, saying it slowly. "That is beautiful, my—"' He stopped when he caught the look I gave him. "I am Ax'ryon, of the Rex'ulti clan."

"Here in Kaua'i?" I asked, as he went around collecting driftwood from the cave.

"I do not know what you mean by Kaua'i. We are on the planet Co'sentyx. Home of the Rex'ulti, Kisq'ali, and Sun'ozi clans."

I furrowed my brow. What was he talking about—another *planet* (one that sounded more like a prescription medication than a place, for bonus points)? Was he crazy, or... How hard did I hit my head when I fell? I mean, here I was talking to a half-man, half-koi dude who claimed I was his mate, and I wasn't diving headfirst into that pool to drown myself. There had to be something wrong with me.

"But how did I *get here*? I'm from planet Earth. One moment I was hiking the side of a mountain in a rainstorm in Kaua'i, the next thing I knew I was falling to my death, and now I'm in this cave. How do you explain that?" I pointed at him as he opened his mouth. "And don't say the fates."

He was on all fours in front of me digging a small pit with his big, clawed hands. He placed some stones around it, then leaned back on his knees. "The fates are known for being mysterious."

I rolled my eyes. "What did I just say about the fates?"

His heavy brow raised. "Our histories tell us there were people from distant planets that mingled with our clans. But those books were written back in ancient times. Generations have passed without any interstellar visitors."

Could I really be on another planet? He seemed so positive.

"But *how*?" I asked again, watching him move around the cave with the gracefulness of a cat. Which was ironic, considering he was more fish than feline. His body was unusual, to be sure, but a work of art—strength and sensuality combined. I enjoyed watching his muscles flex as he leaned down or squatted, his flanks taut, or when he reached and pulled, his arms bulging and his back and abs tense. I was both thankful and embarrassed that he was only wearing the skimpy loincloth. Not that I was much better in just my bra and panties.

"Our histories mention portals," he continued. "But they are always so vague."

Portals. Suuure. That explained everything. I fell through a portal on my way down the mountain.

My God, this was insane.

Ax'ryon continued puttering about the cave as if it was his duty to tend to me. He ripped the driftwood in pieces with his bare hands to get to the dry center. He used two rocks to create a spark and lit a small piece of wood, then coaxed it into a larger flame before setting it in the middle of the pit he'd made.

I rubbed my arms as the heat seeped into my body. "Can you show me these histories?"

He grinned. "As soon as we get out of this cave, I'll show you everything you desire."

I guess getting out of this cave *was* the first step—then I could figure out how to get home. Still, it was nice to feel this cared for and wanted for once. Like Darren would've ever been able to make a fire. He could barely light a match without a big production. The man had never once offered me his sweater even if I said I was cold. Sometimes I wondered why he'd ever wanted to marry me in the first place.

Ax'ryon was off again, gathering more things from the cave —a flat rock, some mushroom-like fungi, and various other plant material. Then after throwing a crooked smile in my direction, he dove into the glowing pool like a sexy eel.

Sexy eel? It's official, I've gone nuts.

I warmed myself by the fire, waiting for him to resurface. In a few moments he emerged from the water, a long piece of golden seaweed in his mouth, two shimmering fish on the end of his spear, and something that looked like a neon green sea urchin in his hand. He placed everything on a rock near the fire and glanced my way. "Are you warm enough now?"

I nodded, and he went back to his catch, neatly gutting the fish with one black claw, then tearing the top off the urchin to reveal the soft center. He slid it all into the fire, as if he'd done this a thousand times before.

"Do you cook often?" I asked.

"It's been a while," he said, poking at the fish with a stick. "We rotate these duties in my clan."

"Between men and women?"

"Between everyone. Including the children." He grinned. "With a little help, of course."

They must function like a commune, sharing responsibilities. Cool. "Where I'm from we tend to have single family units. I cooked, mainly for my ex. Since he never did."

"X?" Ax'ryon's brow furrowed. "I'm not understanding that word."

"Ex-fiancé. It means *former* fiancé. I was engaged to be married."

His nostrils instantly flared, and he leaped up, grabbing his spear near the wall. "Married? As in bonded? This cannot be. I must fight him. To the death." He paced, anger flashing in his eyes.

"Ax!" I said, almost laughing at the intensity of his reaction.

20

"He's not worth the fight. He left me for another woman about a month ago. We were never married. Never 'bonded'."

He relaxed a tiny bit and stabbed the spear into the dirt. "He left you?"

I nodded, suddenly feeling incredibly vulnerable.

"He still deserves death."

I smiled at that, and he sat back down, close enough that I had to shift slightly. My nerves crackled to life at his sudden nearness. He was so imposing: he could have swallowed me whole. I glanced up to catch his gaze, his yellow eyes under dark lashes glowing bright, lined as if by smoky winged eyeliner, but somehow still dripping with masculine, big-dick energy. His tongue flicked over his lips, and I found myself longing to get another glimpse of it. I wondered what it would feel like on my—

"I think the food is burning," I said quickly, smelling smoke.

He blinked and crawled over to it. "It's just a piece of fin catching fire."

"Isn't eating fish like cannibalism for you?" I asked.

He chuckled. "You are amusing, Lee'yah. Fish of the sea, rivers, and lakes might have similar ancestors to me and my people, but we are not at all the same. Besides, they are delicious."

I laughed. At least he had a sense of humor.

As he tended to the food, I studied the fins on his head, back, and tail curiously. They were relaxed now, like how a silk scarf would look floating underwater. But I'd seen what they were like when he was hell bent on killing Darren. They'd stiffened noticeably.

"May I touch your fins?" I suddenly asked. He turned his head in surprise, strands of his glowing white hair settling about his shoulders.

"You can touch anything of mine, anytime," he rasped.

My cheeks flushed. Yes, I was curious to feel an alien body part (cough cough), but another part of me wanted to prove he was truly real, and not merely a man in a movie-quality costume with elaborate make-up. I reached out and grazed my fingers over the fin down his back. It was soft like human skin with cartilage running through it. He groaned and it flared out.

Oh my. I pulled my hand back.

"Your touch..." Ax said, his voice deep and guttural as it trailed off.

Heat pooled between my legs.

This time I touched his shoulder, eager to feel the shiny, scale-like skin that stretched taut over his muscles. It was softer than I imagined. Textured. It felt almost as if I was running my hand over organic chainmail.

"Amazing," I said, becoming aware of his uneven breathing. Was he turned on?

Did he know I was?

"Okay, I'm done." I sat back, hiding my traitorous hands. If I kept this up, I might do something I'd regret.

He raised his nose as if sniffing the air, then swallowed with an aggressive exhale, and turned to catch my eye.

"What?" I said, my voice almost a squeak. I turned away quickly, suddenly overwhelmed with the need to cross my legs as tightly as I could for some inexplicable reason.

Thankfully, he returned to his cooking.

I still couldn't wrap my head around all of this, but at this point I was sure that Ax would keep me safe and warm (hot in some places), not to mention very well-fed. Now, we just had to get out of this cave.

And then what?

6

AX'RYON

LEE'YAH TOLD me she enjoyed the meal I had prepared for her very much. I was pleased to think I could fill her belly, though the more time I spent with her, the more my body ached to satisfy her in other ways. Already, I had scented her arousal in the air, and it only made me hunger for her more.

She claimed not to believe the fates' revelation that we were mates, but in time she would see. She would not be able to fight the intensity of our bond.

Her eyelids drooped as she finished her food. I wanted more than anything to have her doze off in my arms, but I sensed she would refuse. She was stubborn and independent, my mate.

I also wanted to explore the cave to find a way out. I was anxious to get back to my people and introduce them to Lee'yah. They were not used to outsiders, and I knew it could take some time for them to accept her as one of our clan. If not for the bond, I would be wary of her, too.

I suspected that my mother would take the most convincing. We had both expected the Cave of Unmei to show me my destiny as leader, so I foresaw some disappointment on her part. I was convinced Lee'yah would be an able partner in my future reign; my mother might view her as a distraction from my true path as I followed in my father's footsteps.

"Where are you going?" Lee'yah asked through a yawn, as I began to rise.

I grabbed my spear. "To search for a way out of this cave."

"I'll help. Let me come with you," she said, pushing herself up.

"I think you should rest," I said, setting a hand on her shoulder. I reminded myself to be as gentle as I could. I dwarfed her in every way. However, she didn't seem to mind my size as she gazed up at me. If anything, the fragrance of her arousal was intensifying under my touch. I gritted my teeth at the intoxicating thought of her small body so eager and aching for me.

I had to leave.

"I will let you know if I find anything."

"You promise?" she asked, and I caught something dim in her dark eyes.

"I would never leave you, Lee'yah." How could she possibly think I would do something despicable like that? Was it that Dar'ren bastard that made her doubt? If I ever met him, he would be wise to run.

She smiled sleepily, and all the anger I'd felt dissipated. She laid her head down on her balled-up garments, the fiery shadows licking at her tiny face. It was harder than ever to pull myself away from her.

I worked my way slowly around the walls of the cave, searching thoroughly for any gaps or loose rocks. I used my hands and feet to feel for odd depressions in the sandy floor, but nothing showed signs of being an exit or leading to a passage.

There had to be another way out.

As I sat there watching Lee'yah sleep, the pool softly lapping behind her, it dawned on me.

The pool had a current, and fish. It was possible that the

fish came in from the mouth of the cave during high tide, but there were quite a few when I went down earlier and yet, as I peered into the water now, there were none. They had to be going somewhere, possibly to the same place that was the source of the current.

I dove in and swam to the very bottom. It took a while, for it was deeper than I expected. There! Along the pool floor next to the wall, I saw a gap. It was small, but big enough for me to get through. I took the chance and slid through, then went quickly swam to the surface.

I breached in another cave, much bigger and looking to have multiple connecting passageways.

I grabbed an evoki plant from the water's edge. I'd need its bright leaves to find my way back.

7

LEAH

A LOUD SNAP woke me and I panicked, worried I had dreamed the whole thing and I was still falling down the mountain.

After a moment, clutching at the ground, I remembered where I was. I glanced up at the cave ceiling nervously. Nope, not shaking. The sound must've been the crackle of Ax's fire.

I took a deep breath and sat up. This wasn't a dream. I was still here in this cave, with a huge, irresistible koi—hey, where was he?

"Ax'ryon?" I called out. My voice echoed around the walls.

No answer.

I stood and looked around but still didn't see him anywhere.

He promised not to leave me here!

Suddenly, I heard bubbles in the pool, and I braced myself for what might surface.

Ax lifted himself from the water, his body bristling and fins flaring out, reminding me of a dog shaking off the water after a dip.

"Lee'yah," he said with a smile. "You are awake."

26

"You scared me." I put a hand to my chest to steady my breathing. "I woke up and didn't see you. And then I noticed the bubbles in the pool. I thought—"

"Another monster was coming?" he finished, a crooked smile on his face. Once again he came to sit beside me on the rock, even closer than before. You'd think I'd be intimidated, but I really did like how big he was. It made me feel completely safe.

He took my hand, and it disappeared in his large scaly hand. "I promised I would not leave you. You must trust me. Do not worry."

He gazed into my eyes, and I knew he meant it. Who was this guy saying all the right things and following them up with action?

I nodded meekly. "It's been a while since I've been with someone I could trust, that's all."

With Darren's track record of breaking promises, I'd given up on trust, though I'd always held out hope that he'd come around when we were married. I'd gotten used to showing up at family functions or parties alone. I'd gotten used to him making excuses as to why he couldn't go out of his way to do something for me. I knew in hindsight that if it didn't benefit him, he wasn't interested. But knowing that didn't mean it didn't take a toll on my emotions. In fact, sometimes that awareness made me feel even more vulnerable.

Ax reached out with one finger and stroked down my cheek. "Such a shame. You deserve better."

I closed my eyes, willing away the sudden tears, his touch filling me with sweetness and warmth. God, I was a mess. "It's... been a long day," I admitted.

"It's about to get longer, I'm afraid," he said. I blinked back at him.

"Why? What did you find?"

"A way out."

"Really?! Where?"

"At the bottom of the pool."

I blanched. "So how will we get out?"

"We'll swim through."

Was he kidding? I could barely hold my breath on land. I tended to hyperventilate just from watching movies where people had to hold their breaths underwater.

"How deep is it? I... I'm not the strongest swimmer, Ax. And I don't have gills like you. I might be able to make it two minutes max on my best day."

His hand caressed my wrist and arm. I could tell he was trying his best to comfort me. "We'll be quick. I won't let you drown."

"There's no other way?" I asked, letting my head fall against him.

"I'm afraid not. I checked the entire cave. It's this or slowly die here."

I sniffed. "But won't your people come looking for you? Maybe we should wait for them."

"Yes, but I fear the rocks have created an extensive barricade at the entrance. We would likely be dead by the time they made it inside. And we have no idea if this cave is stable. It could settle further at any time, taking us with it."

I ran a hand through my tangled, crusty hair. Gross. That was a mistake.

I knew we had to do this, but honestly, I'd much rather take my chances back up on that mountain hiking in the rain than squeezing through an underwater crevice.

"I'll keep you safe, Lee'yah." He gazed at me steadily, and I couldn't help staring at his lips. They looked smooth, not scaly, and I wondered what they would feel like on mine. I told myself this curiosity was only due to the fact that I could die soon. Again. Still... Shouldn't I kiss him and find out?

No! I had to stop dwelling in the crazy and take a hard break.

Getting out of this cave was my top priority. Nothing else. And to do that, I had to treat today like any other day, with a series of tasks on a to do list. Like back at the office. It was the only way I had been able to move forward when Darren left.

"Okay," I said, getting up and putting on my wet clothes. "Let's do this quickly, so I don't have time to think about it."

Ax grabbed his spear and waited for me to finish adjusting my clothes, eying me up and down. "I think I prefer you without them."

I shook my head and chuckled. "Come on, Romeo, let's go."

He furrowed a confused brow, then shrugged it off and slipped into the pool. I slid in after him.

"Hold me around my neck as tightly as you can. Don't let go for anything. There is room for both of us to go through like this."

I clasped my arms around him, his fins pressing sharply into my collarbone. But I'd rather have that than feel like I didn't have a good grip on him. The rest of my body angled to the side of the fins on his back, and I could feel his tail lift and the fins there brush sensuously against the inside of my legs. *That was no accident, you sly bastard.*

"Ready?" he asked innocently, holding my leg as it bobbed under the water.

I closed my eyes briefly. This was utter insanity. But we had to do it. And I had to trust Ax. "Ready as I'll ever be."

"Take a deep breath...." he said, and as I did, he lowered himself, until we were both underwater. I tried to ignore everything and squeezed my eyes tightly shut, focusing on holding on as he darted downward. He was going as fast as a fucking missile! I forced myself not to count the seconds, as I knew that would only make me panic more. We kept going deeper...and deeper... until I could feel the pressure building in my ears and eyes.

He eased up on the speed, and I finally opened my eyes. It was blurry under the pool, and my eyes stung from the salt water, but I was amazed at how bright it was down here. The water...the plant life...even Ax himself... It all glowed.

I could see the opening directly in front of us and Ax gripped my legs even more tightly against him as he went through it.

The pressure and the lack of air were getting to me. I so wanted to urge him on, but he made his way through painfully slowly.

Then something caught.

No!

He tried again and I felt a tug on my foot. I must be holding us up with something on my boot!

I kicked frantically until I thought I would pass out. Then I felt the tension break. I looked down to see my shoelace in pieces. It must have been torn by the rock.

Ax tried swimming through again and this time we made it.

I needed air. Now!

I pressed my fingers into him as tightly as I could to hold on as we ascended.

Blackness swam in the corners of my eyes, and I fought not to open my mouth and take in water. I began to convulse. I was going to die. For real this time.

My hands lost their grip on Ax, and I drifted.

Time to give in. Time to go to the darkness, floating steadily toward it—

Suddenly I was being dragged through the water, until I felt the sharp, blessed bite of air around me and I landed on the hard ground.

I gulped frantically, the sweet, sweet oxygen rushing into my lungs as I coughed and sputtered.

Strong arms rolled me onto my stomach and pulled me up onto all fours. I spat out water and coughed, feeling like I would never be able to take in enough glorious air.

"Breathe, Lee'yah. Breathe," came Ax's soothing voice as he rubbed my back tenderly.

My coughing finally slowed, and my breathing gradually evened out. "That was close," I huffed, rolling onto my back.

My breath hitched as Ax eclipsed my view of anything else with his huge, powerful body. "But we made it," he murmured, crawling over me, then sliding his hand behind my neck to lift up my head. I shivered, not from cold, but from his scaled hands, the texture igniting fiery tingles all over my skin. My heart had already been beating fast from our narrow escape, but now it wouldn't stop as he gazed at me, hovering there, his expression filled with so many things—concern, curiosity, and above all desire...

I swallowed, eyeing his lips again. Before, I'd backed off from kissing him, knowing I had to focus on survival. But now, we'd made it out of the cave. Time to seize the moment and move on to my second priority.

His eyes darted to my lips, and I lifted myself up, crushing my mouth to his.

He growled, his hand tightening around the back of my neck, and I gasped at the thrill of it. When he swept his tongue into my mouth, my entire body swooned, and I moaned from somewhere deep and forgotten.

He ran the back of his finger up the side of my neck and grasped my jaw, teasing my lips with his, then sliding his tongue over mine. *Ridges*! His tongue had so many delightful ridges!

Our mouths danced together and I panted, desperate to get closer to him. I wanted to feel the scrape of his claws, the roughness of his scales, and the slick, ribbed pressure of that tongue... everywhere.

As he lowered his weight, his hard cock pressing against me like a massive steel beam, my body trembled with need. I whimpered, writhing under him, almost drunk with desire.

"Lee'yah," he said hoarsely, before ravaging my mouth once again.

Why did I put these stupid shorts back on, anyway? Why did I need clothes at all? I wanted to feel Ax completely. I wanted his thick koi-man cock rubbing against my clit and then thrusting deep within my pussy.

A tug at my ankle told me he was trying to take off my boots. Yes!

But then something long and wet with what felt like dozens of sticky suction cups on it wrapped around my calf. Uh... What was he doing?

I pushed at Ax's chest.

"What?" he rasped, his eyes hooded with lust.

That's when I realized both of his arms were around me.

Fuck.

"Ax!!" I yelled as I was torn from his grasp and dragged to the edge of the pool.

He finally reacted, confusion on his face as I was plunged back into the water.

8

AX'RYON

W͟ʜᴀᴛ ᴊᴜsᴛ ʜᴀᴘᴘᴇɴᴇᴅ? One moment Lee'yah was underneath me, locked in my embrace, the next, she was gone with a scream.

I jumped up and hurled myself back into the pool with my spear.

There in the water, Lee'yah was fighting with Ty'zir and his many vexatious tentacles.

Meddlesome wretch.

I grabbed her and gave Ty'zir my fiercest roar. He would feel the end of my spear if he didn't let go of her this instant.

He dropped her immediately, and I pulled her back to the surface, helping her out of the water.

"What the fuck was that?!!" she yelled, getting to her feet and scrambling to the opposite side of the cave. "He was like half-man, half-octopus!"

Ty'zir emerged from the water, his thick, rolling tentacles pushing him onto the sandy cave floor. "Sorry! Sorry! I was just playing!"

I groaned, trying to control my anger as I scrubbed a hand over my face. "Lee'yah, this is Ty'zir, my Kisq'ali brother. He

33

lacks any kind of social skills and has spectacularly terrible timing."

Ty'zir threw me a look and crossed his bulky arms. "My timing is impeccable. I just thought I would have a little fun. I saw you two zooming through the pool, then got an eyeful of this one when I surfaced." He waggled his eyebrows.

"Watch it, Ty," I threatened. "Lee'yah almost drowned just a few minutes ago."

His onyx eyes widened in alarm. "Oh, my apologies, Lee'yah. I meant no harm."

Lee'yah was still backed against the wall, her mouth open as she stared. "You... You don't have legs," she stammered. "Or a lower half... well, except for the...the..."

"What language is she speaking? I can't understand her." He lifted one of his tentacles and waved it around. "Is she staring at these?"

"She's not used to seeing creatures like us," I explained. "Lee'yah is my mate."

"Ax..." Lee'yah warned.

"You bonded?! And on your twenty-fifth star cycle, too! Congratulations, brother." He slapped my back with a tentacle, then studied Lee'yah, a little perplexed. "But... What is she? She doesn't look like any of our clans."

"She's human. From the planet Earth," I said.

"She's from a different planet? Could this prove our histories true?"

"Possibly. We're still not sure how she got here." I smiled, recalling our first meeting. "She was unconscious in front of the cave when I found her, then the cave entrance collapsed after we'd taken shelter in it. We were stuck together. It seems the fates fancy themselves comedians, much like you."

"Funny," Ty deadpanned, rolling his tongue over his teeth.

"How did you get into the pool?" I asked him.

"There's another opening under the water toward the east. It leads out onto the Lryxii shore."

"Hmm... I'm sure the opening is deep down?" I said, looking doubtfully at Lee'yah.

Ty nodded. "Very deep."

"Yeah, don't even think about it," she said, shaking her head firmly. "I'm done with underwater passages."

I cursed. "Lee'yah doesn't have gills," I explained to him.

"I noticed." He looked her up and down. "But she sure is beautiful."

I beamed, regardless of how much I disliked the way he was ogling her. "I know."

Lee'yah's cheeks flushed, though she kept rubbing her arms. She was clearly cold and perhaps more than a little confused. "I'm planning to take her through the passage that heads out into the Hexzif forest."

"I'd wait until morning. It's dark now and you don't want to run into any Sun'ozi scumbags," Ty replied.

"True. Thank you, brother." I smiled at him and we pressed our forearms together.

"Sorry to interrupt." He winked at me and flipped his long white hair back. "But... Gods, she's tiny. How will you—"

"Good*bye*, Ty," I interrupted, nudging him with the handle of my spear.

Ty grunted, sliding sideways. "Okay, okay... So long, Lee'yah." He waved at my still-gaping mate. She blinked and waved back hesitantly as he slithered back down into the water.

9

LEAH

"That was...interesting," I finally said after Ty disappeared.

I was still in shock from battling what I could only describe as a kraken. My mouth was dry from hanging open so long when I had been staring at his lower half—all eight colossal tentacles of it. I wasn't really sure why I was surprised. Before this, I'd been making out with koi-man, and I had *really* liked it.

If I'm not on another planet, I definitely need to be committed.

"Did he hurt you? Do you need more evoki plant?" Ax asked, fretting as he inspected my body anxiously, his hands feeling every inch of me.

"What is an evoki plant?" I asked.

He went over to a glowing plant and plucked a stem of it off a rock. "It's what I used on your skin wounds before. The balm inside soothes and heals." He tore it open and squeezed blue gel into his palm, then came over and rubbed it into my skin.

As much as I felt completely out of place on this planet, I had to admit that it fascinated me to no end. Fates that bonded two souls together...luminescent plants with healing gel...half-

36

human half-sea creatures, some of which treated women like queens...this world was wild, and I'd only seen a corner of it so far.

"I'm sorry you had to meet Ty that way. He's always a jester, but he is truly a loyal friend."

"Oh, I'm fine now," I said, laughing and batting his hands away as he slid them under my clothes. "It was just...surprising. And I've had enough surprises for today."

"I'll make a fire and get you fed." He began doing everything he had done before again, gathering more driftwood and catching a seafood dinner for us. I couldn't deny that Ax was impressive. I appreciated that he knew what to do and just did it. The doting was pretty nice, too.

I had no clue what time of day it was, or even how long the days lasted here on Co'sentyx. That, combined with the lack of light and familiar surroundings (oh, and an alien suitor), had me completely turned upside down.

But yes, I was hungry again. Probably all the swimming.

As soon as Ax had the fire going I sat down on a rock to remove my boots and socks.

"What happens after we get out of this cave?" I asked as he served us more fish.

"I take you back to my village and we begin our life together." He said it as if it was the most natural thing in the world.

"Ax, you do know I have to find a way back to my own planet...right?"

He bristled, his fins flaring out as he chewed his food. "Why? From what you've said, it sounds like your people do not cherish you the way you deserve to be. This ex of yours, as you call him, should have been tossed into the ocean and left to drown."

I smiled at the image of Ax punting Darren into the sea. "But it's my home."

"We will make you a new home." His eyes met mine steadily. "You will be my partner in every way. Your wish, my command. I will see to your every need."

My cheeks heated, and I sighed. "Wow. That's not the way it often works on Earth."

"It doesn't sound like anything works very well on Earth," he grumbled, then washed his face in the pool.

I didn't know what to say to him, how to explain that fate didn't play a part in our decisions on Earth when it came to partners. Sure, there were those who believed in soulmates, but I wasn't one of them. Still, the more time I spent with Ax, the more I wondered if there might be something to this whole fated mates business. Especially considering my poor luck back home.

"You may feel differently about me as time goes on," I said glumly. "Darren did." And, well, every one of my past boyfriends, too.

He reached down and pulled me up, his hands threading through my hair as his thumb stroked over my lips. "Impossible. Darren was a fool. You're perfect, Lee'yah. May I show you exactly what it means to be *mine*?"

Oh my... The hunger in the bright depths of his eyes had me melting in his hands like a gelatinous pile of evoki goo.

I knew my answer, and fear rushed through me at the thought of it, because I knew what it might mean for both of us.

"Yes... Show me..." I breathed, helpless to fight it any longer.

He groaned and took my mouth with his, swiping his ridged tongue over mine, and I received it with fervent hunger. I grabbed at him, relishing the feel of the silky-slick scales on his arms and back. I wanted to touch every part of him, from the gills on his neck to the hidden parts under his loincloth.

His claws got caught on my clothes and he cursed. "Get out

of these," he commanded in a raw voice, gruffly pulling at the seams of my tank top. I would never deny him anything if he said it like that.

I pulled my top up and over my head, tossing it aside. His mouth went to my neck, sucking and kissing its way downward. I let my head drop back as he teased at my shoulder and collarbone, his lips somehow rough and soft at once, his tongue's ridges adding even more complexity to the sweet mix of sensations.

He tugged impatiently at my bra strap, and I hurriedly reached behind me to release the clasp. His fingers tangled in it and ripped it off in a second.

A growl fluttered in his throat as he squeezed my bare breast, and I trembled.

"Ax..." I whispered, as he urged me down to the slate and sand below.

"I do love it when you call me that," he purred, his breath hot against my chest.

Heat swirled between my legs as he dragged his tongue over my nipple, the ridges doing exquisite things to the sensitive nerve endings. When his mouth closed around my breast, I cried out, my fingers knotting in his hair.

He sucked and licked my other breast as I arched beneath him. "Yes," I moaned.

Then he moved down further, kissing my stomach and nipping at my navel, exploring and tasting every exposed part of my body.

I let go of him to undo my shorts. In seconds, his hands were in them and at my panties, tugging everything down in rough, jerky motions. He snarled, and it was obvious he wanted them off as much as I did.

With all my clothes gone, he sat up and grabbed my legs, hooking them over his shoulders. Almost upside down, my shoulders barely touching the ground, my naked body was entirely exposed to his roving hands. I felt helpless and vulnerable, entirely at his mercy. And it turned me on like you couldn't imagine.

"Your scent is making me delirious," he said, inhaling deeply. His face was dangerously close to my pussy. But instead, a large deft finger slid into my folds and stroked me. My sensitive flesh throbbed, as he circled my clit, making me writhe and moan.

"You like that, my Lee'yah?" he purred. "My finger teasing your aching cunt?"

I panted. "Yesss." Who knew aliens would be so good at dirty talk?

"Gods, you're wet." He took his finger away and I heard him putting it in his mouth to savor. He moaned, then ran his wet finger over my breasts, caressing my nipples.

"More, Ax," I pleaded, whimpering, my body desperate for him.

"You want more?" he echoed, his voice hoarse. "Then my Lee'yah will have more."

He grabbed my thighs and lifted me higher, until I felt the electric zing of his ridged tongue as it delved into my folds. His mouth descended on my pussy, slowly licking and sucking every sensitive spot, making me shake and whine. I couldn't keep still, the movement of my body only increasing the sensations that scrambled my nerves until they short-circuited into a frenzy of pleasure.

Both of us were loud, me with my cries and moans, and Ax with his snarls and growls, like a wild beast feasting on his prey.

"I could devour you," he groaned, holding onto my thighs with such force I knew I'd be bruised tomorrow. But hell, it was worth it. His mouth and tongue were sending me over the edge fast. I didn't want him to stop. Ever.

"Ax... I'm going to come..."

"*Yes*, explode all over my blessed face," he growled, as his tongue swirled again and again over my clit.

My whole body trembled and shook until the tension released in a massive eruption.

"*Fuck!*" I screamed, seeing stars. It only seemed to spur him on, making me quake harder, jerking and convulsing as I moaned.

"Lee'yah," he murmured into my pussy, the vibration a soothing end to my climax.

Ax eased up, licking me gently and sweetly, slowly releasing my thighs, letting my legs unhook from his shoulders and supporting me as I slid down. He hastily shoved my discarded tank top underneath me before I touched the sandy cave floor.

"Your skin is so fragile," he said, seeing how it had turned red where he had been holding onto me. "Did I hurt you?" He used his mouth and tongue to kiss each bruise and mark.

"It's a good kind of hurt," I replied with a contented sigh.

As soon as I had caught my breath, he pushed my legs apart and lifted my hips to meet his pelvis. He ripped the leather pouch off his raging cock, which stuck up high and hard in the space between us.

His pupils were dilated, and he might have looked terrifying to anyone who didn't know what he had just done to me. But I knew that sexy secret.

"I need to be inside you," he growled.

"Wait," I said, leaning forward. "I want to see you and touch you first."

He nodded, biting his lip as if in pain. "Quickly," he said, as I ran my fingers over his long, thick length. He had no scales here, nor on his balls. Just smooth, fleshy, white skin that was nearly translucent. Much like you'd expect on a koi fish, actually. The shaft was not overly girthy, nor was the head particularly bulbous, but he was hard and well-shaped for pleasure. I stroked him gently, enjoying the weight of him in my grasp.

"Your touch will ruin me, Lee'yah," he said through gritted teeth. "If we don't hurry, I'm going to burst all over your pretty little hand."

I smiled. "Next time," I said, rubbing the clear fluid already oozing from his tip over the head, then guiding him to my opening.

10

AX'RYON

I snarled and circled her sweet slit with the slippery head of my cock. "I can tease, too, my Lee'yah."

She bit her lip, sweat beading on her brow, her eyes hooded. I had satisfied her with my tongue, the music of her moaning my name still in my ears. And gods, I wanted to do that again... but I also wanted to fill her up and claim her once and for all as my own.

I wished I could sink my fingers inside her to stretch her first, but my claws would cause her pain. And with the way she raised her hips eagerly to meet my probing tip, I knew she was ready. I took aim and slid into her hot, dripping wet cunt.

"Fuck," she whined, her eyes wide.

"Lee'yah?" I asked, when she began panting in shallow breaths.

"I'm okay, you're just big. Like, *really* big."

I grinned. "We'll loosen you up. You're soaking my cock, and it's...exquisite."

I adjusted my position, straightening one of her legs up to rest again on my shoulder. I held onto her lithe limb and drove forward, kissing and nibbling on her toes.

"Mmm....oh," she purred, clutching at my thighs. She felt like a warm rainstorm, a million droplets streaming over my body, teasing the nerve endings, squeezing and caressing my cock as I thrust in and out of her.

"You're breathtaking," I groaned, our cosmic bond solidifying as we moved together.

She made such beautiful, mind-melting noises, I knew I wouldn't be able to last much longer.

I leaned forward to grasp her luscious breasts and whip my tail around to use the soft end fin to caress first one taut nipple, then the other. She cried out and I plunged into her deeper.

"Ax!" she whimpered. "I'm so close." Her eyes followed my tail fin as it teased her breasts.

"Yes, my Lee'yah, come for me and only me."

She arched and I felt her sweet body shiver and shake, shattering into a million pieces as I continued to drive into her. She screamed my name and her cunt spasmed around my hard, aching cock until I lost all control, my seed blasting from me like a volcanic eruption.

I roared, my body flexing and tightening to near pain. But my cock could have fallen off and I wouldn't have cared, for I had reached the pinnacle of pleasure with my mate, and nothing would never be the same.

11

LEAH

"You awake?" Ax whispered against the shell of my ear, before running his tongue along it and placing a soft kiss on my neck.

"If I wasn't before, I am now," I replied with a happy sigh, curled up in his arms.

We'd spent the entire night drifting to sleep only to wake and explore one another all over again—from sweet, teasing orgasms to pulse-pounding explosions that had left both of us breathless and sore.

It was a night filled with new, mind-blowing experiences, but also deep, emotional connections. Somehow, I felt as if I'd known him forever. I'd thought that would unnerve me, but instead it just filled me with a strange combination of satisfaction and excitement.

He ran a claw over my arm. "What are these markings?"

"They're called tattoos," I replied. "They are made by putting ink into the skin with a needle."

He made a clicking noise. "Is it painful?"

"A little, but tolerable."

"Then why do you do it?" He rubbed at my shoulder, as if testing the permanence of the ink.

"It's art, an expression of yourself on your skin."

"So they have meaning," he said, turning my arm around and pulling it up. "Wait. Is this what I think it is?"

"I was wondering if you'd notice." He'd found the red koi fish tattoo running down the back of my arm, the face curling around the top of my shoulder.

"It's beautiful. What made you want to get this?" he asked, caressing it with the back of his finger.

"I had just graduated from college and I traveled to a country called Japan with some friends. The guy at the tattoo shop said the koi fish symbolized strength and perseverance. And for some reason I was really drawn to it."

He sighed. "There are so many things in what you just said that I don't understand. But I must say, the color is striking, and the symbolism suitable for you."

"Not as striking as your coloring," I replied. "And thank you."

I felt the smile on his lips as he nuzzled my neck. "You flatter me."

"Never," I chuckled, lazily running my fingers over the scales of his forearm. His skin was fascinating to me. The scales were dry, but always slick and shiny, as if they were wet.

"Do you need water to survive, like a fish on Earth?" I asked.

"Yes and no. Rex'ulti can go fourteen sun cycles without submerging, but it's not pleasant. After a week, we begin to show signs of dehydration...flaky scales, sore joints, listlessness."

"What about Ty'zir?"

"You mean the Kisq'ali? They can only go seven sun cycles before they are near death."

I whistled. "Damn, so they all live close to water?"

"Yes. There is an extensive settlement of caves and sea huts on the Lryxii shore. The Rex'ulti and Kisq'ali have been allies for ages."

"Okay, so who are those Sun'ozi you were talking about earlier?"

"Land dwellers," he grunted, and I could hear the disdain in his voice.

"Like me?" I asked, curious. "What do they look like?"

"They have your humanoid form, but are covered in a leafy green skin, and have vines sprouting from their backs that have a dangerous reach." He palmed the center of my back. "They have flowers growing from their heads, but don't let that fool you. They are rotten to the core."

"Tell me how you really feel," I quipped, but he just continued, my joke lost on him.

"The Sun'ozi are petulant bullies, bitter that the Rex'ulti have been in power and ruling the land territories for hundreds of star cycles. They'll tell you it's not fair, but truth has never been their strength. My clan continues to reign due to our prowess in combat, our solid alliance with the Kisq'ali, and successful community initiatives."

"You must really love your people." I could see how his chest puffed out in pride when he spoke of them.

"I do. And all I've ever wanted was to be their leader. I came to the Cave of Unmei on my twenty-fifth star cycle hoping it would show me that future."

And then I came along instead. "But why do you need a cave to tell you that? You already know it in your heart. If it's obvious even to me that you'd be a fine leader, I'm sure your clan sees it."

His arms tightened around me. "You are wise, my Lee'yah."

I relished the warmth and safety I felt with him.

"In any case, the cave showed me something much better."

He nipped at my ear. "I can't wait to introduce you to my people."

"How do you know they'll accept me?"

"Oh, they won't at first. I'm sure they will be suspicious of you. It will take time."

My heart sank. "And your family?"

"My mother and I are all that is left from my line. She's my biggest supporter. She's dreamt of my future as leader almost as long as I have. She can be stubborn at times, but I know you'll win her over."

He said it with such conviction. I wanted to believe him, but I had serious doubts. What if I came between Ax and his mother? What if I ruined Ax's chances to live his dream? It sounded like his clan was everything to him. What if they never accepted me as his mate? I could never make him choose. And if he did choose me, what's to say he wouldn't ultimately come to resent me for it?

No way. I'd already been dumped for holding Darren back, I did not want to get in the way of Ax's dreams as well.

Tough as it was, I knew what I needed to do. I had to go back home to pick up the pieces of my shattered life and leave Ax to his destiny. Staying here was putting his life's dream too much at risk.

My insides twisted in pain, but I ignored it.

"So we just go through that passageway?" I asked, changing the subject. I pointed to the offshoot of the cave.

"Yes, just a short way through leads to the forest."

I looked around, trying to get my bearings. "Where was the entrance of the last cave?"

"Around the sentinel rocks to the west, facing the shore."

I shook my head. "My sense of direction is all mixed up here."

"I'll teach you," he replied with a smile. It made me sick

inside to hear his sweet enthusiasm as I secretly planned my escape.

He got up and reached down to lift me to my feet and left his arms around me. "I'll catch us a meal. You go get dressed."

He smacked my ass and leaned down to kiss me deeply, and I reached up to hold his face. I would miss this...plus his constant desire to feed me.

He stared at me lovingly as he put his loin pouch back on, then dove into the water.

Now was my chance.

I dressed in a hurry and ran toward the passageway. Taking one last look back, I mentally thanked Ax for everything he'd done for me, trying not to let tears cloud my vision. Then I turned and didn't stop until I saw light. I quickly made my way through the rocky opening into the forest.

The light blinded me at first, but soon my eyes adjusted. It looked very much like a forest on Earth, only brighter, with unusual flora and fauna. There was what sounded like the chirping of birds from somewhere above, and it smelled fresh and dewy. The colors were more vibrant, and even the soil on the ground seemed to shimmer, along with the bark on the trees.

I walked to the right, since that would be west. I'd just follow the rocks until I hit the shore, as Ax said.

I'd only gone a short way before I heard something. An animal? No, I heard speaking. Could it be Ax? I didn't pause to listen; instead, I climbed up the rocks as far as I could and hid in a small pocket out of sight. I peeked down at the area below.

Four men (well, not men as I knew them to be—they were green with vines sprouting from their backs) were down below, talking. I could just make out their words and for some reason I could understand them.

"Let's go back, I'm hungry," one of them was saying,

49

kicking a root. He was thicker around the middle than the others, but still pretty darn buff. They were all Herculean. What is it with this planet and gigantic man-monsters?

"What's new, Pa'kol? You're always hungry," another laughed, and Pa'kol made a gesture that had to be their version of 'fuck you' behind his back.

"No, he's right, we should go back to the village. We've already collected enough biostyk stems for at least thirty sun cycles of treatment." The one that spoke carried a large green sack. "That should suffice for our punishment."

"Dumb that we even had to do this, just for spiking the gavae juice at the last hunt celebration." He shook his head. "Gar'ek can be such a tyrant sometimes. We were only trying to have some fun."

"Well, don't let him hear you say that. He'll hang you upside-down from the trees in the square and let the kids pelt you with mygar squash. Like he did last star cycle."

They laughed at the one who glared back, flipping his braided twine-hair over his shoulder angrily.

"Mmm, mygar squash," Pa'kol murmured dreamily, and they all groaned.

They had just started walking further into the forest when one stopped.

"Did you hear that?"

I pressed myself back into the wall, holding my breath. Had they heard me?

"It sounds like footsteps."

"Hide!" One of them whispered. "Someone is coming."

And they all dispersed into the forest, instantly disappearing into the foliage, as if they were born to do it.

"Lee'yah!" the voice called, and my heart dropped with a thud. Ax. "Where are you?"

No! Why did he have to follow me? He was walking directly

under where I hid. I desperately wanted to warn him, but then we'd both be sitting ducks for the Sun'ozi.

Vines suddenly flew out and began wrapping around his body.

"Get him!" the Sun'ozi men yelled, as Ax roared.

At first Ax batted at the vines, trying to fight them off. But once his spear was torn from his hand, he was soon overpowered. There were simply too many of them.

"What is the meaning of this?" he snarled, as the four Sun'ozi approached, smug looks on their faces.

"We're taking you back to our village. Gar'ek will be *so* pleased with our catch."

Ax struggled in the grip of the vines around him. "Just one more reason for my people to attack yours."

They all laughed. "Without their best warrior to lead them? We'll see."

"Once again the ones without gills will rule the land. Our time has come! Sun'ozi!" They raised their weapons high in the air in unison.

Shit. This was bad. I had to get to that beach and search for the portal, but how could I possibly leave Ax to these guys? What kind of person would I be if I didn't at least try to come to his aid? All he'd done since I arrived was help me.

I sighed as the plant guys began dragging him away through the forest.

Only when they were safely out of sight did I slide out from my hiding place and climb down to the ground.

To my right was the way home.

Straight ahead, I most amazing man I'd ever met.

I took a step. Then another.

I wouldn't look back. I'd just keep moving forward.

12

AX'RYON

BACK AT THE SUN'OZI VILLAGE, I sat in a thatched cell, fuming. It smelled like sour soil and mineral moss in here. My captors said Gar'ek was out hunting with another group but he'd be back within the sun cycle to see what they had captured.

I'd already tried cutting the twine ropes enclosing the space when my guards weren't looking, but they were too thick, even for the sharpest parts of my claws and teeth.

What did it matter, anyway? Without Lee'yah, they could do whatever they wished. I didn't care what happened to me. My people would survive. They had flourished before I existed, they would flourish again.

My only worry was that they had captured Lee'yah as well, that she had wandered out to the passage only to be snatched by these brutes. They swore they had no idea what I was talking about when I mentioned a female, and although they could be lying, I knew their tells. Plus, I would have heard her if she was somewhere nearby. She wouldn't let them take her without a fight. I loved that about my mate.

But if they didn't have her here, where was she?

Anger flared inside me. The Sun'ozi were stupid, but not

completely so. They wouldn't kill her: she would be too much use to them. I ground my teeth at the thought of my mate suffering at their sticky, greedy, dirty hands.

I knew they hadn't done anything to her yet. I would've felt that in my heart. And every so often I swore I caught her delicious scent in the air.

At the moment, however, her scent was overpowered by the smell of cooking meat. My stomach growled.

"Can I at least get something to eat?" I asked Jik'tar, the bigger and more brutal of the two guards they had watching me. The other one had gone to get them food.

"Ha!" he barked. "You're lucky you still have teeth, fish breath."

"My clan will remember your mistreatment and disrespect of me."

"Yeah? Your clan can shove it up their scaly asses."

Suddenly, a *definite* whiff of Lee'yah drifted into my nostrils. I looked up just in time to see something fly at Jik'tar.

"What was that?" he roared, as the object hit him in the face.

I couldn't help but laugh.

"You shut up," he said, then turned back to where the flying debris had come from. "Who threw that? Who's there?"

When nobody answered, he snarled and took another look back at me. A rock came at him next, hitting him on the back.

"That's enough!" he yelled and stomped off around the corner.

I listened carefully. It sounded as if he fell, his cry cut off by a loud thunk.

What was going on? I stood, pressing myself against the rope bars, waiting. Then Lee'yah appeared before me, her eyes wild.

"My Lee'yah!" I said, trying to keep my voice down.

She was magnificent, standing there with a huge stick in one hand and a key in the other. The sight of her like this would be burned into my memory forever.

"What happened? Did they take you?" I asked, as she hurriedly came over to the cell and worked at the lock tied into the twine ropes.

"Um...well..." she stammered as the lock disengaged and the flap opened. I grabbed her, gathering her to me, kissing her mouth, her face, and her golden hair as it shone in the sunlight.

"My sweet Lee'yah," I sighed, her body filling me with renewed energy.

She returned my kiss with fervor, until I reluctantly tore myself away. "We must go; the other guard might return at any moment."

She nodded and I took her hand, pulling her through the forest.

"Where are we going?" she asked.

"To my village," I said, as we rushed between the trees.

"Wait! I must talk to you."

"Now? At least let me get us out of Sun'ozi territory."

"Okay..." she acquiesced, and we continued along on a worn dirt path. After a while I found a small thicket of trees where we could hide.

I gathered her close to me, never wanting to be apart from her without the touch of her skin and the heat of her body.

"Did they harm you? Defile you? Tell me. No, don't. It would drive me mad with rage." The words fell from my mouth fast and frenzied.

She touched my face. "No, they didn't hurt me. They didn't even capture me." She paused, taking a deep breath. "I left the cave. I left you...to try and find the portal back to Earth."

Her words stabbed me in the heart, and darkness tinged the corners of my vision.

"But I heard them and hid. And I could understand what they were saying as easily as I can understand you when you speak Co'senti."

"Why would you leave me?" I asked, searching her eyes for answers. They were glassy with tears.

She took a shaky breath. "Your future would be much easier with a Rex'ulti mate, one who would fit in with your family and your people. If it ever came down to it, I would *never* want you to have to choose between me and the destiny you've always dreamed of. You'd just end up resenting me for it and I couldn't deal with that kind of heartbreak. Not again, and especially not with you, Ax." She sniffed, tears pouring down her cheeks.

Seeing her cry made everything inside me hurt. I curled my finger under her chin and tipped it up until she had no choice but to look me in the eye. "You could never come between me and my destiny. You are *part* of my destiny now, Lee'yah. My mother and my people will know this. It might take some time, but they will see it on my face and feel it in their hearts."

"But—"

"I am not Dar'ren, nor anyone else who broke your trust. I always keep my promises. And I promise that I shall never resent any choice I make when it comes to you." I took her hand and placed it flat on my chest. "This beats for you now, Lee'yah."

She closed her eyes. "Ax..."

"So, although it pains me to do so, I will take you to try to find the portal, if that is what your heart desires," I finished.

Her eyes went wide. "What? I don't understand."

"You are my mate. No matter where you go or what happens, I will always be bonded to you. I will do whatever it takes to make you happy, even if that means we are not together." It would tear me apart, but I had to do the honorable thing. For her.

She was openly sobbing now, and she threw herself at me, burying her face in my chest.

"I can't...I can't..." she said, the words muffled against my body.

"Cannot what?" I asked, holding her tight.

She turned in my embrace and wiped her eyes. "Can't leave you." Her entire body shuddered. "I want to stay here with you. You're the best thing that's ever happened to me, Ax."

"You don't want to go back to Earth?" I asked, excitement creeping back in.

She shook her head and wiped her eyes with the heel of her hand. "In an ideal world, I could keep you and go home, but I'd choose you over all of it now." She gazed up at me, her face still wet. "You make me feel like the most special person in the universe. You care about what I think, what I feel, and you treat me like a queen." She smiled deviously. "You're also incredibly hot and know how to satisfy me like no man I've ever known."

I bit my lip, pride puffing out my chest.

"I'm so sorry I doubted you and ran away. Never again. I promise."

"I feel like I'm dreaming," I replied, my heart beating faster.

She chuckled. "Welcome to the club. You were right. There's nothing back on Earth that makes as much sense as us. No matter where we are, I want to be at your side, Ax."

I nearly burst with happiness.

"But I still don't get why I was able to understand the Sun'ozi when they spoke Co'senti." She gazed up at me, eyes searching for answers.

I shrugged. "I'm not sure. Maybe it's simply what the fates needed you to understand."

She gave me a knowing smile and I kissed her, pressing in as close as I could without hurting her. It just wasn't ever close enough. I wanted to lay her down in the grass and show her just how happy I was then and there. "I'm sure about one thing, though. You're mine, Lee'yah."

She looked into my eyes and clutched at my face. "And you're mine, my mate."

And my heart soared higher than the tallest trees above.

KRAKEN
MINE

INTERSTELLAR PORTALS BOOK 2

JINX LAYNE

1

KAIA

MORNINGS HAVE ALWAYS BEEN special for me.

From the day I could stand up on a surfboard, my dad and I would wake before the sun—and before Mom—and head down to the North Shore in his trusty pickup to shred the morning waves. It was our time to bond over the surf, the sand, and a big cup of serious Hawai'ian coffee.

After Dad passed, I continued the tradition.

Mom moved out of our small cottage to live with my auntie Urima closer to the bay, but I stayed and kept the old pickup running.

Some mornings I'd much rather sleep in and pad around the house sipping my dark blend, but disappointing Dad was out of the question, and if I didn't want the rest of Kaua'i joining me out on the water, I had to get there early. Besides, my job giving surf lessons at the Princeville Resort required me to be there by 8am anyway, or the tourists got antsy.

The salty breeze was starting to kick up as I got out of the truck, but it was still warm enough to hit the water in my favorite black bikini. I pulled off my t-shirt and shorts, then grabbed my board, tucking it under my arm.

A lewd whistle carried on the wind and caught my attention.

My gaze flew across the parking lot to where Makaio and his motley crew of friends were leering at me as they loitered by his truck. "Pilialoha," he muttered, loud enough for me to hear. Well. Slut wasn't the worst thing he'd called me since we'd gone out a few times over six months ago.

I could go and find another beach but screw that. Makaio didn't get to tell me where I could surf just because he was an asshole. This was *my* beach, damn it. I would *not* let him scare me away.

I fingered the shell necklace my dad had given me as a little girl.

I won't let him control me, Dad. Not for making one unfortunate mistake.

The group continued to glare, but I squared my shoulders and jogged toward the water.

"That's right. Run away, hookamakama," Makaio yelled after me, with jeers from the boys.

I had no time for trash like him or his loser friends.

When I hit the shore and felt the wet, crunchy sand under my feet, I didn't look back. Straight into the water I went, paddling out as far as I needed to get to the best waves.

The water was cool, but not cold. It woke me up almost as much as the coffee I'd had earlier. I got up into my cobra pose position over the choppy waves closer to the shore and stayed like that until I had to duck dive under the larger ones, just like Dad had taught me. When I was as far out as the rocks, I straddled my board, waiting.

I scanned the shore. Makaio hadn't followed me, thankfully, and neither had his dumb friends. I wasn't sure what I would do if they came after me in the water.

Why couldn't he just leave me alone? Hadn't he done enough?

Suddenly, the swell of a wave caught my eye just behind me, like the hunched back of an enormous sea monster rising up under the water.

Go time.

I pressed my body forward, paddling hard.

This was going to be a big wave—I could feel it.

I jumped up and planted my feet on the board, balancing as the crest formed, the foam beginning to roll.

Riding a wave was like flying, and my board was the vessel propelling me onward. I zigged and zagged, just enough to keep me from getting too far into the tube.

For the first wave of the day, I was stoked.

Thanks, Dad.

Makaio and those idiots would *not* be ruining my day.

Not now. Not ever.

2

TY'ZIR

MORNINGS COULD SUCK my sixth tentacle.

I crawled out of my bed and slid into the sea water on the other side of my dwelling, my body thirsty after the long drought of night.

My eyes were still blurry from sleep as I blew bubbles under the water, stretching out my aching limbs, and grumbling.

I swam out of the cave passageways quickly. I didn't want to run into anybody today.

Not after yesterday.

It had been the anniversary of my twenty-fifth star cycle, and I'd gone to the Cave of Unmei—or what was left of it after the recent rockslide—to meditate. It was tradition for warriors in our clan to visit the cave on that day to have their destiny revealed.

But surprise! No destiny for me.

I'd waited and waited. In the cave. Outside the cave. Near the cave.

Nothing.

The cave gave my best friend, Ax'ryon of the Rex'ulti clan,

64

his mate last star cycle. He hadn't even wanted one! Although he was very happy with her now, of course.

Me, that's all I wanted.

Especially after I saw Lee'yah, Ax's mate. She was a human from a planet called Earth. We figured she arrived here through a portal somewhere near the Cave of Unmei, mentioned in our planet's histories.

Lee'yah was beautiful for a being so wildly different from me and Ax. She had two legs, like Ax and his Rex'ulti clan brethren, and our Sun'ozi enemies. But no gills to breathe underwater like the Kisq'ali and Rex'ulti, or vines that sprouted out of her back like the Sun'ozi. Her hair was golden, her skin tanned and smooth. She was tiny and wonderful...

And all for Ax.

I was beyond jealous. I wanted my own human female!

I had never developed strong feelings for any females of any clan on my planet. Besides, they all lusted after warriors, anyway. And now the Cave of Unmei had failed to deliver a destiny to me, and the fates had spoken: I was no warrior.

Whatever. I'd known that in my heart a long time ago.

I sat on the shore, my tentacles dangling over the wet rocks as I munched thoughtfully on a piece of seaweed with the spray of the water misting over me with every crash of the waves. What was that? Something had caught in a crevice below me. I reached in and found a necklace of some sort, made from shiny black rocks and white shells. Curious. None of the clans made jewelry like this. I did not know what it could be, but I liked the look of it, so I stowed it in my azarashi skin satchel for safe-keeping.

I sighed. If I'm not a warrior, what am I?

Lonely, that's what.

I looked out over the waves, searching the horizon for answers.

And then something appeared.

A figure with arms and legs, flying over the waves, standing on a flat surface with fins. Could that creature be riding...a *fish*?

As it got closer, my heartbeat sped up. It was a female.

My body lurched and I nearly choked, my heart slammed against my chest so hard.

My mate.

I could see her more clearly as she got closer. Her dark hair was flying in the wind, her body firm and strong, graceful and barely covered, as she balanced on the waves. Gods, she was magnificent.

Without another thought, I launched myself off the rocks and into the ocean.

I zoomed toward her as fast as I could until I was next to the finned board—aha, not a fish after all—careening along with her.

Breaching the surface of the wave, I propelled myself up with my tentacles.

"Helloooo my beautiful mate!" I yelled over the water.

When she saw me, her eyes widened and she lost her balance, falling backward into the wave. The board kicked up and followed, almost as if it was attached to her. Could it be part of her body? Her feet, perhaps?

I dove down, desperate to prevent her from striking the rocks below.

Underneath the surface, she was bobbing like a jellyfish. Her limbs were slack, her eyes were closed. Gods... Was I too late? Had she hit the rocks?

The ocean dragged her further down and pulled her side to side with each swell.

I grabbed her; the board followed and smacked against me as I sped for shore.

I growled as I pulled her up onto the sand and laid her down.

She didn't move, but I could see she was breathing. I touched her tanned skin and groaned. She was so soft and warm, and my fingers ached to touch more of her.

Her body and features were very similar to Lee'yah's: she had to be human. Except my mate's hair was dark as kazan rock, and long, splaying out like seaweed around her. And her skin was darker than Lee'yah's, more the color of evoki bark than burak hide.

As I checked her over for injuries, my entire body thrummed with need. My tentacles vibrated as they moved over her supple skin.

The board was attached to her ankle by what looked like a long, thin, black...limb? Or could it be a vine? As I inspected it, I realized the cuff was not part of her ankle, as it rotated without touching her. I pulled at its two ends, and it made a horrific tearing noise as I freed it from her. Still, as I felt her ankle with my kyuban, I could tell her ankle was injured. Their suction tubes could detect flesh abnormalities. I needed healing items.

As I studied the surrounding space, I suddenly noticed that everything was...different. From the washed-out blue of the sky to the drab-colored sand, rocks and leaves, it was all very dull. Looking further inland, I gasped.

Strange dwellings such as I'd never seen before were everywhere!

Odd bits and pieces and unusual items dotted the beach and ocean rim.

I didn't understand.

Where did all of this come from?

I suddenly heard voices, the language something other than Co'senti, and when I scanned the shore I saw figures in the distance. More humans, maybe?

Lee'yah had told me humans feared strange beings, and generally regarded them as threatening. She also told me they had never heard of my or Ax's kind.

So I took my mate with me, and I hid.

3

KAIA

My eyes fluttered open as I felt a soft caress trailing down my cheek.

"Morach subarashi najir," came a deep, soothing voice.

Oh wow. Was I dreaming? A man—an incredibly handsome one, at that—was hovering over me, the sun framing his face like an angelic halo. Silvery eyes, a devilish smile, a square jaw. Long silvery-white hair hung down over a smooth, built chest, and unusual striped tattoos that almost glowed covered his shoulders and lean arms.

Who was this hottie? And what language had he just spoken to me in?

There was something familiar about him, but I couldn't place it. Like I'd seen him in a dream, maybe.

Suddenly a dark, dusky blue tentacle rose up behind him.

"Look out!" I yelled, though it came out more like a croak.

He frowned and turned, following where my finger was pointing.

Then I saw another tentacle come up...and another.

I pushed up onto my elbows as he backed away.

Holy...

My mouth opened to scream. But nothing came out.

The hottie had no legs. Okay, he did have a bottom half... but it wasn't like anything human.

Instead, he had eight thick tentacles, the size of beefed-up elephant trunks. Like some half-man, half-octopus creature.

I *was* dreaming! I had to be.

I tried to get up. Dream or not, I had to get away. Who knew what this guy wanted to do to me?

"It's all right, morach najir." He held up his hands.

I sat down again. That first bit was English. And he did seem to be trying to calm me down...

But there was no calming down when my eyes dropped to his tentacles as they rolled and slithered in the sand.

He followed my gaze and quickly coiled them up tightly underneath him. Was he trying to hide them from me? Good luck! That would be like trying to hide a hippopotamus under a bathmat.

Regardless of this creature's attempts to make himself less frightening to me, I needed to get out of there. I got to my feet again. As soon as I had my footing, I yelped, pain shooting through my ankle.

Octopus-man rushed forward and held me steady in his arms.

What was wrong with me? Why wasn't I screaming? Why wasn't I pushing him away or fighting him off or...*anything*?!

He eased me down with my back against a tree trunk, using his arms and tentacles, which wasn't quite as weird as I thought it would be. I still whimpered at his odd suction-like touch, though, and he immediately tried to tuck them away again. Then he spoke again in that calm, yet throaty voice.

He pointed to my ankle. "Hurt."

I nodded. Yes, my ankle was hurt.

He then mimed surfing, crouching with his arms out for

balance, pointing at me. It was really hard not to be distracted by his lower half; the tentacles were joining in on his miming efforts. He framed his face and smiled, then mimed me falling, flailing and closing his eyes with his head tipped to the side and his tongue out, as if floating helplessly in the water.

I couldn't help but grin. This was all so absurd. I was playing charades with a kraken-man.

Oh! He was the one I saw in the water next to me!

Now I understood why he didn't need a board.

He mimed me screaming and I couldn't help it: I burst out laughing.

He stopped and smiled at me, and my *God*, that sexy smile went straight to my core.

Who was this beautiful creature?

We gazed at each other like that for a moment until he shook it off.

"Heal," he said, nodding toward my ankle. Then he moved over to rummage around in the surrounding foliage.

His lower half moved like an octopus on land, his tentacles slithering and rolling over each other. They were not as slimy as a sea-creature's, though. And they were clearly very powerful, strong enough to raise his top half to maybe eight feet. He towered over me, and I was pushing six feet.

He returned to my side with some large, waxy leaves, plant stalks, and flowers. He laid the waxy leaves flat and ripped open the plant stalks to squeeze out the sap. Then he mashed the flowers and the sap together on the leaves with a rough stone. Once that was done, he wrapped my ankle with the leaves, watching my face carefully as he tightened them, concern over my comfort written in his silvery eyes.

"Good? Yes?" he asked.

"Yes. Good," I replied, nodding. "What is your name?" I

asked as he was tying the leaves around me with a long piece of vine. I pointed to him.

He shrugged. "Name?" He squinted, as if struggling to place the word.

I pointed to myself. "My name is Kaia."

He furrowed his brow.

"Kaia," I said, patting my chest.

"Kaia," he repeated. "Subarashi," he purred.

"Subarashi?" I asked. "That is your name?"

He smiled and pointed at me. "Kaia subarashi." Then he pointed to himself. "Name Ty'zir."

"Ty'zir," I said, nodding.

He reached out and slid his fingers under my chin. I shivered, but not because I was cold.

"Kaia morach subarashi najir," he rasped, like it was the most romantic thing in the world to say.

I believed it. He had me sagging into his gentle fingers. "Okay."

I'd never seen a man beam back at me like he did.

4

TY'ZIR

THE CAVE OF UNMEI had finally shown me my destiny, thank the gods.

And my mate, Kaia—such a lovely name—had agreed to our bond! My entire body buzzed with excitement. I longed to pull her into my arms and hold her, touch her, kiss her, fill her with my cock and my seed. I yearned to pleasure her until she screamed my name, her voice becoming hoarse from her moans.

But not yet. For now, she was hurt and needed my protection while she healed.

I didn't want to scare her. Didn't want her to feel rushed. And I really wanted to be able to talk to her properly.

Lee'yah had only taught me a few English words and most of them had fallen out of my brain the moment I laid eyes on Kaia.

We'd have to perform the bonding rite that would enable us to understand one another. I could only hope the rite would work on another planet. Because this was definitely Earth. I must have breached the portal, no idea how.

I slid my hand to the side of her neck, my thumb against her jaw. She tensed but didn't resist, her dark eyes searching mine.

73

When I took her other hand and placed it on my neck to mirror my position with her, she jerked away. Had she felt my gills? Did they frighten her?

"Whatareyoudoing?" she said. I did not know what the words meant.

"Please," I whispered, hoping she'd feel the bond's pull.

She didn't fight me when I placed her hand back on my neck, though I could feel the tension in her body under her skin. Gods! Her scent, her touch, everything about her consumed me. I prayed I could get through the bonding rite without making a complete fool of myself and drooling all over her.

I leaned in and her breath caught. She moved away slightly.

"Easy, my mate. This won't hurt. It will feel incredible, and only make things better between us." I knew she didn't understand me, not yet, but I could tell she liked the sound of my voice by the way her lashes lowered.

I leaned in again, slowly pressing my forehead to hers. A long sighing breath escaped her mouth, and I had to fight not to suck it into mine.

May the gods be in our favor...

As soon as we were connected, I could feel the power building. Balls of electric heat unfurled within us. *Yes*!

She nuzzled against my palm, a soft moan escaping her lips, and I nearly lost it. I wanted to press her entire body to me with a possessive growl right there and then.

Gods, I could feel her heart beating along with mine. And then I felt something more. Her loneliness, the betrayal by her kind, and her yearning as it mingled and swirled with mine. It filled me with an intense emotion and insatiable desire for her and only her.

"My beautiful mate," I whispered. "You are mine." I stroked her cheek.

Her eyes flew open. They were dark and rich, like shimmering tidepools at sunset. "What did you say?" she asked, and I understood her.

It had worked!

"I said, my beautiful mate," I repeated, gazing down at her.

"Mate? Wait, why can I understand you? You weren't speaking English before. Well, not entirely."

"We're bonded now."

"Bonded?"

"Yes. After mates perform the bonding rite they are enlightened with what needs to be known."

She swallowed. I could see the confusion all over her pretty face. "Ty'zir," she said—and hearing her say my name made my already thundering heart skip around like a lovesick burak—"what the hell is going on here?"

I gave her my most winning smile.

"It's a long story, and I don't think we should stay here while I tell it. We're not safe from being discovered. I hear humans don't always do well with those that are different from them."

"You're a little more than just different." Her eyes traveled over me. I loved how that felt. "What... What are you?" she asked.

"I'm of the Kisq'ali clan, from the planet Co'sentyx, and I somehow made it through the portal on my planet that connects it to Earth, and um...vice versa." That was the simplest explanation I could think of.

She blinked at me. "This is some crazy ass dream."

"I think we must both be awake." I smiled. "I've never seen a female as beautiful as you in my dreams."

"Aww, Ty," she said, a lovely blush creeping over her cheeks.

The familiar way she shortened my name had my lower regions clenching. This woman...

"It's the truth," I replied simply. "You're breathtaking."

She fondled her throat almost nervously and coughed. "Yes, well, enough of that." She waved her hand. "You're right, we aren't safe here. We need to get back to my truck. I guess I'll take you to my home."

I smiled. She wanted to take me to her dwelling? "What's a truck?"

"A vehicle for transportation. It's parked not that far away. See all those vehicles over there? But it's parked in a lot with too many people around right now." She gestured to my lower half with her head. "They'll see you. I'll go ahead and then wait for you."

"Can you walk?" I asked.

She held out her hand to me. "Let's see."

I pulled her up to a standing position and she stepped forward with her bad ankle. She winced.

"I can limp at least." She lifted her foot in the sand and examined it. "The wrap you made is snug and really helps."

"It's similar to what we use back home for sprains and fractures, but your plant-life here is different than on Co'sentyx so I had to improvise."

"You did well," she said, making me beam and puff out my chest.

"You're my mate. It's my job to protect you in any way I can."

"Yeah... About this mate thing..." she began, but approaching voices sounded nearby. "You should go," she whispered. "Get into the water and wait until the beach clears. My truck is the small red one with a bunch of surf stickers on it."

"Stick-ers?"

"Never mind." She waved me off. "We'll put you in the back and cover your lower half with beach towels."

She had completely lost me by this point, but I trusted her.

I stole a kiss from her cheek before turning and going back out to sea.

5

KAIA

I SAT IN MY TRUCK, pondering. What in the actual hell was happening?

One moment I'm surfing, totally tearing it up out there, having one of the best rides of my life, and the next thing you know I'm waking up next to an alien...admittedly a very hot one...claiming he's my mate.

Honestly, I should peel out of here as fast as possible and go straight to the hospital to be evaluated. Why else would I be considering helping an alien who's half-man, half-octopus to hide out in my home? A legit kraken!

And yet, for some reason, I trusted Ty. Unless that bonding thing was just a spell he put me under, to make it easier to subdue me for his nefarious plans which might or might not include eating me.

No... He was too gentle and too kind for that.

He saved me! Sort of. I mean, I only fell off my board because of him. But then again, he pulled me ashore and wrapped my ankle, using only things from nature to heal me. Who does that?

Aliens, apparently.

I waited patiently at the shore for this heartthrob of a creature to make his way to my truck so I could whisk him away to safety. But then what?

Every so often I gazed out at the ocean and saw him bobbing there, waiting for the coast to be clear, looking like a regular guy taking a swim. Okay, maybe more of a verifiable beefcake than a regular guy. It made my heartbeat speed up just to think about him and his touch.

What was up with this bonding business? I wouldn't have believed such a thing possible, but then again, suddenly we could understand one another. I knew I was still speaking English. And when he spoke, his mouth was forming words from another language that just seemed to click in my brain now.

Could this whole mate thing be real?

I scanned the shore and realized no one was around. The parking lot was empty as well. Thankfully, Makaio and his stupid friends had been long gone by the time I came back to the truck.

I saw Ty coming up from the water, and I got out of the truck. If anyone saw him, they'd probably think he was in costume or part of some animatronic show. He'd attract a crowd for sure. Good thing he moved lightning fast.

Watching closely, I noticed he only used four of his tentacles to "walk" over the ground. I guess the others were used for manipulating...other things. My body flushed, thinking about what kinds of things those tentacles could do. God, I needed help.

Just as he made it to the truck, a car pulled into the parking lot. Ty used the truck bed as a shield, casually leaning on it with his elbows and waving at the people. They waved back with a hang loose gesture which he returned. Quick recovery.

As soon as they were otherwise preoccupied, he took my hand.

"Hi," he said, caressing my wrist, staring deeply into my eyes.

"Hi," I breathed, goosebumps running up my arm from his touch.

"You put on more garments," he said, eying me up and down.

"Yeah." I'd put my shorts and t-shirt on over my bikini.

"A shame," he said with a wink.

My whole body heated in an instant. *Down, girl*.

He was one to talk. He wasn't wearing any clothes either! Only a small brownish satchel strapped across his body. Not that he had anything to cover up, really.

Anyway, I didn't mind seeing his muscled torso in all its glory, put it that way.

"Get in," I finally said, patting the truck bed invitingly.

"Anything for you, my mate." He gazed at me lovingly as he climbed in, the truck shifting with his weight.

I covered his lower half with as many beach towels as I could find, then got in the driver's seat and opened the back window.

"Hold on, Ty," I said, as I started the engine.

"May the gods help me," Ty mumbled.

6

TY'ZIR

Confession time: riding in the back of Kaia's truck was *not fun*.

Trees, dwellings, people and more odd things than I could count flew past us at a speed I'd only ever managed to reach in the water.

There was the swerving, and a constant up and down, and then the stopping and starting. My stomach lurched with each movement.

But I wouldn't complain to my Kaia. She was taking me to her dwelling! I'd crawl over the sharpest shards of sea-shells to get there if I had to...or be tossed about in the back of this vehicle.

By the time Kaia stopped, I was nauseous and dizzy.

"How was it?" Kaia asked, lowering the small end piece of the truck.

I tried to give her my best smile, crawling out slowly. But then my stomach roiled, and I pushed past her, speeding toward the bushes.

"That good, huh?" Kaia said, as I retched.

I wiped my mouth and turned back gloomily, holding onto the back of the truck for support.

"We don't have trucks on my planet," I explained, panting. *Thank the gods.*

She pressed her pretty lips together. "Sorry."

"Don't be," I said, waving her off. "We made it." I looked around us curiously at the dwelling. "Is this your home?"

A small building with a pointed roof and yellow and white walls sat nestled among green foliage and unusual flowers in muted hues of purple, white, and red.

"Yes, this is it. It's not much, but I inherited it when my dad passed. My mom wasn't happy that he left if to me and moved in with my auntie."

"It's wonderful, my mate." I touched her arm. So her father had died and her mother moved away? I fought the need to take her into my arms. "But I'm sorry for your loss. I would have liked to have met your father."

She smiled at me. "I have a feeling he would've liked you." She pulled me along to where a few wooden steps, like those in the Sun'ozi villages, led up to a platform, covered by another flat roof, where there was a door. She opened it, and indicated I should enter, but I stopped when I saw the clean interior.

"My tentacles are filthy. I shouldn't drag the outside into your home." It didn't feel polite, or even civilized.

"You're awfully considerate for a kraken," she said, smiling.

I gave her a nervous smile. What was a kraken?

"Hold on a sec—I have a hose." She limped slowly to a spot on one side of the dwelling that had a long green vine. She attached one end of the vine to a spigot on the wall and turned something with her hand. Water instantly spewed from the other end of the vine. Absolutely amazing!

"Lift those up," she said, spraying the water over my tentacles.

I lifted, letting her wash off the sand, sea, and other particles I'd picked up along the way.

"Can I see?" I asked, curious to hold the vine.

She handed it to me, and I turned it to spray the water into my mouth.

"Wait!"

Too late. I'd already pressed the handle, spraying my entire face with a hard burst of water. Drenched, I handed her the vine and swished around what little had actually gotten in my mouth.

She was laughing. I loved the carefree, melodious sound of it.

"Perfect," I deadpanned, my face and hair dripping.

Still chuckling, she turned off the water and tossed me a towel that hung near the door. I dried off as best I could, then followed her, crouching and sliding my way through the door.

Once inside, my gaze bounced everywhere. So many things! Like on the trip up here, I couldn't comprehend it all. It was too much to take in. The floor, the walls, the furnishings were all so foreign. Light came both from the outside and from magical fixtures above. Images and designs hung on the walls and various items were placed around the room. I had no idea what purpose they served.

"Why don't you try having a seat on the couch," Kaia said, closing the door and locking it as she peered out into the front garden.

"Couch?" I repeated.

"That big green thing in front of you," she said. "It's for sitting on."

I glanced at the long rectangular object that lined the wall and jutted out to the left. She came over and sat on it to show me.

I moved my tentacles over it and lowered myself experimentally. It was soft, pliable. Comfy! I tried to recline, but my elbow slipped on the edge, and I only just caught myself from falling.

Smooth, Ty'zir.

She giggled. "This must all be so strange for you."

"Just a little." I arranged myself as best I could.

She got up and went into the room directly next to the one with the *couch*. "Would you like a drink or a snack? What do you eat? Please don't say human flesh."

"Gross," I grimaced. "You're a clever girl. I'm sure you can guess."

She turned to me, pursing her lips in thought. "Seafood?"

He grinned. "Indeed. Mostly fish, crustaceans, fruit, plants...anything we can find, really, that isn't too difficult to prepare."

She opened the doors of a big gray container with a light inside. She pulled out items, then did the same with a compartment above.

"I'm vegan, so I don't have any seafood. But I have nuts, berries, and pineapple."

"Vee-gann..." I repeated, rolling the unfamiliar word around my mouth.

"That means I don't eat things with or from anything with a face."

"Interesting," I said, watching her bustle around the space.

She brought over bowls filled with nuts I'd never seen before, small dark berries, and yellow chunky triangular pieces of fruit. Then she hefted a container of water onto a wooden platform with four legs in front of the couch.

I pulled off my satchel, placing it on the ground next to me for safekeeping.

The nuts tasted like kija nuts, the berries like miko berries, and the fruit, well, I couldn't think of anything similar on Co'sentyx. It was as delicious as a godly ambrosia.

"I could eat mountains of this," I said, popping another triangle into my mouth, savoring the intense explosion of flavor.

She grinned and poured a container of water for me. "Glad you like it. It's called pineapple. We have tons of it here in Kaua'i. Oh, and the nuts here are called almonds, and the berries are blueberries. Because they're blue, I guess."

As delicious as the food was, I knew Kaia would taste a thousand times sweeter on my desperate tongue. Hrmh... I downed some cool water to calm my nerves. My cock would burst from its internal pouch if I didn't get myself under control.

She pulled her shapely legs under her and reclined. "Now: tell me everything."

I took a breath and began with how Lee'yah and Ax'ryon met. How Ax had found her on the beach near the Cave of Unmei on Co'sentyx one star cycle ago, his twenty-fifth.

I told her about Co'sentyx and the three clans that lived there: my clan, the Kisq'ali, who lived in the sea caves off the Elder Rock; the Rex'ulti, our allies, who lived in land dwellings, but were also seafaring with gills and fins (I explained that they had legs like hers but with webbed feet); and the Sun'ozi, our enemies, purely land-dwelling, with their leafy appendages and vine-sprouting bodies.

"The Sun'ozi are not fond of the other clans because our warriors constantly vanquish their attacks. They've had their chances to rule, and they get greedy each time. They have proved they can't be trusted with power."

She crunched on a handful of nuts thoughtfully. "So, where do humans come in?"

"There are tales of other beings that lived among our clans long ago, but so many generations have passed since we had any visitors that we thought those records were perhaps untrue.

Then Lee'yah came along. She said she had fallen off a cliff when she was on a dangerous hike."

"Kalalau trail?" she asked.

"Yes! That's it!"

"That's near here. But a fall off the more dangerous parts would typically be fatal." She chewed on her lip. "Maybe she fell into the sea, and it swept her out into the portal?"

I huffed. "But I saw you as I sat on the rocks this morning. I couldn't have gone through any portal until I went out after you."

She tapped her forehead, staring past me. "And if the portal is right where I was surfing, I would think others would go through and end up in Co'sentyx."

Yet we'd only had Lee'yah show up for ages. This was truly a puzzle. "Could it have something to do with the Cave of Unmei and mate bonding?"

Her eyes narrowed. "You said that the cave can show you your destiny, but Ax wasn't in the cave when he found Leah, and neither were you when you found me."

I sat back, getting more accustomed to the couch. "Could mate bonding be separate from the Cave of Unmei's destiny?"

Kaia crossed her arms. "Maybe. But what exactly is this mate bonding, anyway? Here, fate is mostly only in made-up stories. Typically, in real life, we just meet someone, and if there's an initial attraction, we spend time with them to find out more about who they are and if we are compatible. If we are, we fall in love."

"Sounds like a lot of work," I said.

She laughed. "Now that you put it that way... It is. And often, it doesn't even work out after all of that."

"Have you ever fallen in love, Kaia?" I asked, not sure if I wanted to know the answer. I wanted to be the one she fell in love with. The first one. The only one.

She shook her head. "I've dated, but nothing serious."

"Fools..." I whispered, secretly cheering inside.

She squinted at me. "How did you know I was your mate, though?"

"When I saw you riding the waves, it was as if you had snatched my heart from my chest. I had to be near you, to touch you—" I stopped, not wanting to scare her. "A warm, soft glow of desire ignited inside me, and a desperate longing followed it."

Her expression turned introspective as she nibbled on a wedge of pineapple.

"Do you not feel that way about me?" I asked, a lump suddenly in my throat.

She licked her lips, and I found myself nearly hypnotized by the sensual movement.

"I wouldn't say that..." She appeared to be choosing her words carefully. "I feel the inklings of the longing you describe, but my practical side tells me it's just physical desire. I've felt nothing like this before, though. This entire experience has been surreal."

I gulped. There was hope. Knowing she did not feel the mating bond as strongly as I did was somewhat disheartening, but I would not back down from a challenge. I would show her the pleasure I could bring her and open her eyes to her fate.

She was my mate.

Mine, and only mine.

7

KAIA

"WHAT IS CO'SENTYX LIKE?" I asked, thinking about Ty and this bond. There it was again: the inferno that raged inside me like an ocean of heat whenever my thoughts turned to him now. I was way too young for hot flashes. Could this be the mating bond?

"Vivid colors, clear skies, pristine lands," he said, biting into more pineapple, the juice making his lips glisten. Though sexy to watch, I was worried he was going to make himself sick if he ate much more.

"And quiet," he continued. "We live a simple life, sharing responsibilities to keep the clan safe and healthy."

It sounded really nice, actually.

"What strife there is comes from warfare between the clans. The Sun'ozi believe they should rule the lands, since they are what they call 'pure' land-dwellers. They are in constant battle with the Rex'ulti. The Rex'ulti won't stand by and allow themselves to be mistreated, and we support the Rex'ulti in every way."

Grr. It seemed that fighting existed anywhere that groups of beings gathered. Why was it so difficult for people to get along?

"Are you a warrior?" I asked.

"Would that impress you?"

I shrugged. "Not necessarily."

"Good, because I'm not a very good warrior. I'd rather entertain the warriors than fight alongside them."

"I can believe that. You're naturally funny."

"Funny-*looking*," he said, making a face.

"Ty, come on," I laughed. Even making a face, he was stunning. "You're gorgeous. There is nothing funny-looking about you. Trust me."

A slight pink color tinted his cheeks, and he suddenly found one of the buttons on the couch cushion fascinating.

"You could make a lot of money with your face."

He furrowed his brow. "What's money?"

Oh, wow. "We...uhh...exchange it for goods and services. The more you have, the more stuff you can buy. Anything from the most basic food to exotic getaways around our planet."

"Fascinating," he said. "But—what if you don't have very much of this *money*?"

"Your life is extremely hard." I sighed. "Honestly, the system you have going in Co'sentyx sounds much better."

"Maybe, but not if you're not there. I'm not going back without you, Kaia."

"Ty, it's not safe for you here," I groaned. "If they find you, they'll take you and keep you, probably experiment on you, or torture you for information. You don't want to spend your entire life hiding, do you?"

He leveled his silvery gaze at me. "If that's what it takes to be with you, then yes."

I couldn't believe how completely serious he was. He reached out and put a hand over mine, my body coming alive at the simple touch.

"You don't even know me, Ty."

"But I do. When we performed the bonding rite, I could feel you. The loneliness you carry in your heart, and your hope for better things to come. I want to take away everything that hurts you and give you all the happiness in my soul. Even if I have to sacrifice everything."

I looked up at him, my eyes filling with tears. Only one other person had ever made me feel like he would fight the world for me. And now he was dead.

"Who are you?" I said, tears spilling down my cheeks.

"Your fated mate," he whispered, as he gathered me into his arms.

My mind reeled as I nestled my face against his neck, inhaling his sweet and salty musk.

"Tell me," he said, stroking my hair. "Tell me about this loneliness that plagues you."

I hesitated at first. Bringing it up always made me feel everything all over again. Things I'd rather forget. But Ty made me feel so special and safe. And I wanted him to know every deep, dark secret about me.

I sniffed. "I dated a guy from here in the neighborhood, Makaio, for a couple of weeks. It wasn't long before I realized it wouldn't work out. He had a bad temper and was super controlling."

I felt Ty's muscles tense under me.

"So, I broke it off. He got angry, called me names, and ever since he's given me a hard time when we see each other."

Ty's breathing intensified, and I could tell he was struggling to keep it together. I pressed my face lower into his chest, curling into him.

"And then... My period was late."

"What does that mean?" he asked, cupping the back of my head.

"I didn't menstruate on time." I wondered if his species procreated in the same way humans did.

"Oh," he said uncertainly. Then, "Oh!—I think I understand."

I took a deep breath. "I wasn't ready to have a baby. Especially not with Makaio." I remembered back to how difficult it had been to work out on my own. I'd made a mistake trusting Makaio when it came to birth control. But I wasn't about to let it dictate the rest of my life. "Ultimately, I decided to terminate the pregnancy."

He held me tighter, but didn't speak.

"Someone saw me at the clinic where I was having the termination done and word got around. I lost my friends and family over it—even my mother never looked at me the same way again." I inhaled a shaky breath. "And Makaio and his friends were the worst of all. Though I'm sure Makaio's anger stemmed more from his bruised ego—knowing I wanted no part of him, including a child—than anything else."

Ty's hands combed gently through my hair. "Where was your father through all of this?"

"He had died a few years before."

His thick arms squeezed me again. "I'm so sorry, my mate. I'm sorry you had to go through that alone. And I'm sorry your friends and family couldn't respect your decision. I can imagine how betrayed you must feel."

I let the tears fall down my cheeks, silent sobs wracking my body.

Ty held on tight, whispering sweet words of comfort as I cried in his arms.

Soon I felt his lips drop to my eyelids, my cheeks, my hair—kissing me, nuzzling me. Somehow, this stranger knew exactly what I wanted, what I craved.

Respect. Comfort. And love.

Eventually I stopped crying and realized I was kissing him back, my mouth on his neck, exploring his face, my hands in his hair. Fevered and urgent, I suddenly couldn't get enough of him.

I was hungry. Needy.

Finally, I pulled him into a proper kiss, my mouth pressed flush against his.

He paused, possibly surprised, then groaned.

He tasted like pineapple and sea salt, and my tongue dove into his mouth seeking more of his sweetness.

He moaned long and loud...and his tongue...it felt like a soft sea urchin, with spongy, almost prickly feelers, teasing my mouth.

I choked as I considered how that tongue would feel on other parts of me.

"Kaia?" Ty asked, backing away from the kiss. "Tell me if I'm too eager. I can't resist tasting every part of your hot mouth."

"It's fine," I said. "But stick out your tongue. I want to see it up close."

He obeyed.

It looked like a normal pinkish human tongue, except when I put my finger on it, dozens of tiny feelers probed and caressed. When he closed his mouth to suck on it, the sensations only intensified.

"Holy mother of..." I finally pulled my finger away. "That tongue is *dangerous*."

He waggled his eyebrows. "I can't wait to run it over every delicious part of you."

Me either.

He pulled me close, and as I went back to kissing him, something thick and hard pressed against my thigh. I ground myself on his stiff rod.

"Sweet gods," he rasped into my mouth. He moved his kisses to my jaw and down the column of my throat. That crazy tongue blazed a fiery trail across my skin.

"I want you, Kaia. From the moment I first saw you, I wanted you."

I was swimming with desire, need, lust, whatever you wanted to call it. Something deep and primal was stirring awake within my soul, as if he had a direct connection to my aching core.

"I want you, too. All of you." I didn't care that he was an alien with the lower half of a kraken. I was ready for it.

He growled. "Can I use my tentacles?"

"I said all of you, didn't I?"

With that, his tentacles were pulling my shirt up and over my head, then flinging it aside. As his mouth and tongue trailed down my collarbone, he untied my bikini top.

The soft suction tubes on the underside of his tentacles supported my back, and I leaned into them, like a crazy, wicked chair.

Suddenly, his palm was kneading one breast while his mouth kissed over the other. When his tongue sucked at my peaked nipple, those tiny feelers electrifying it, I moaned, fists clenching in his hair. The tentacles at my back lowered me down to the sofa as he moved his mouth over to my other breast, making my toes curl.

As I let go of his hair, he kissed down my belly.

Fuck, this was already insane.

Two tentacles crept over my breasts, the sucker tubes teasing and tasting my nipples like so many velvet mouths. I arched into them, my hands coming up to caress their smooth sides, soft like the hide of a seal, with baby fine hairs. They vibrated under my touch, sending a whole new wave of sensation over my sensitive skin.

His two other tentacles made fast work of my shorts, then did the same with my bikini bottoms. For someone with no experience with human clothing, his tentacles knew how to remove them with ease.

The cool air touching my now bare skin was electrifying enough, but when Ty's searing tongue touched my pussy, I nearly shot through the roof. "Oh God!"

"You taste like my new favorite meal." His breath was hot against me, teasing my flesh as his tongue went to work, driving me out of my mind. Those adventurous feelers touched parts of me long forgotten and now had them buzzing with desire and need.

"Yes..." was all I could manage.

As he devoured me bit by torturous bit, two tentacles continued to torment my breasts, and now another two began creeping around my thighs, coaxing them wider apart. More velvety sucker tubes teased at my inner thighs, behind my knees, and my toes. The sensations overwhelmed my body in the best possible way, and within moments, I was panting, riding toward the edge of the pleasurable cliff.

My orgasm crept up my legs, making them tremble. "I'm going to come, Ty," I moaned.

"Yes, my sweet Kaia. Come for me," he growled. A finger slid inside me and curled next to that unbelievable tongue.

Every inch of my body was spasming and coming completely undone.

I yelled out my release, my heart pumping like mad as waves of pleasure washed over me—tentacles, tongue, and finger drawing my climax out so long that I thought I might collapse from exhaustion.

His tentacles went from teasing suction to more of massaging motion, and he finally removed his mouth from my throbbing pussy, trailing kisses over my thighs and up my stomach.

When I let out a long breath, Ty removed his finger and sucked it into his mouth, his eyes closing as he savored it.

"Your sweetness is addictive, my mate."

I smiled, my eyes trailing down his chest, past his navel, to where the skin of his tentacled half began. Just below, where the human pelvis would be, there was a huge bulge, as if something was pressing from underneath his skin.

"...Is that what I think it is?"

8

TY'ZIR

MY EYES FEASTED on her beautiful naked body.

Dark eyes hooded. Tanned skin glistening. My tentacles still wrapped around her limbs and that sumptuous cunt swollen and wet from my mouth pleasuring her to orgasm. I could not taste greater happiness. Just knowing I had put that sexy, sleepy grin on her face made my entire existence.

"If you think it's my cock, ravenous for your cunt, then yes, my sweet. It is exactly what you think it is."

She giggled and sat up, and I unrolled my tentacles from her body, already missing the feel of her skin under my kyuban.

She ran her fingers over my bulge. "How do I get at it?"

I brought her hand to my seam. "This seam loosens and opens when I'm aroused."

"Like a cock pocket?" she asked. I snorted.

"If that's what you want to call it."

She caressed the seam, and I shivered as it released. Then those enchanting fingers dipped inside and wrapped around my cock, tugging it out into the open.

Her eyes went wide.

"Is it too big?" I asked anxiously, panicking at her reaction. "I don't want to hurt you. I still don't know how Lee'yah and Ax—"

She put a hand to my lips. "It's perfect. You're perfect. We'll make it work, even if it takes a while." She stroked her hand up my shaft and I groaned, plasia seeping from my slit.

She ran her finger over it. "Pre-come?"

"We call it plasia. It lubricates."

"It's slick like KY Jelly, a product we use for lubrication."

"Human males don't make their own?"

"They do, but often not enough. And many men don't take the time to stimulate a woman to help her get properly lubricated."

I shook my head. "That makes me sad for human females."

"Me too." She smiled, continuing to fondle me, my body jerking in response. "You're so hard and smooth. It feels like the snout of a dolphin, but slightly flexible."

"I'd be interested to see this dolphin you speak of." My breath caught as she stroked my pale blue cockhead, swollen to its maximum size. I couldn't get the image of her hot, wet cunt out of my head.

She leaned forward and kissed the tip of my leaking cock.

"*Kaia*—by all the gods in Tingokku—"

I gasped as her tongue slid out to swirl over me. She delved into my slit and I bucked, grabbing her head with a growl.

"No. If you do anything more with that mouth of yours, I'll lose all control—"

As if to defy me, she took me into her searing mouth, impossibly deep, and slowly crept her tongue back up.

I cursed, trying not to send my release down her throat.

"Kaia, please," I begged.

When she pulled off, her eyes were dark, her pupils fully

dilated. She climbed forward. "Let me try taking you inside me. I need it now."

Once again, her words had me teetering on the brink.

Gods, this woman!

"Do you have protection?" she asked. "I don't know if I have any condoms here. It's been a long time."

"Protection against what?" I asked, pulling her closer.

"Pregnancy, or sexually transmitted disease," she replied.

"Hmm... We don't have any diseases like that on Co'sentyx. And as far as pregnancy goes, Kisq'ali males don't produce viable seed until they have released around five times."

"Really? Over how much time?"

"About two day cycles, but it depends on the amount of ejaculate with each orgasm. Some males produce more. So four to five times is normal."

Her eyes were wide. "This is wild. Human men produce viable seed from the get go."

"Our job as males is to make sure the female is pleasured. She won't stick around to take our seed otherwise."

Kaia laughed. "That makes sense, I guess. What if you're mated already, though?"

"The same physiological rules apply."

"Good to know," she said, then kissed me as she lifted herself over my dripping cock, the plasia now covering it completely.

I held her up with my arms and tentacles as she guided my cock into her small opening.

When she had managed to slide just the head in, I almost fainted. Literally. Her cunt gripped me so tight I blacked out.

"Ty,' she breathed, and brought me right back to life, as more plasia helped her ease me inside. More and more of my cock disappeared into her hungry, deliriously hot cunt.

A snarl rumbled from my throat.

She grabbed my shoulders and ever so gently, ever so slowly, pumped up and down, biting her lip and moaning my name.

It was both beautiful and maddening; my mate using me for her pleasure, driving me insane, my cock pulsing along with the beating of our hearts.

She threw her head back, and I slid my tentacles over her neck, chest, and behind her ear.

"Yes, my mate," I murmured, mesmerized as I watched her enjoy me. I'd wanted a mate for so long and had received the most perfect one in every way.

I would thank the gods for all of eternity.

She grabbed the tentacle sucking at her neck and stuck her tongue inside one of the kyuban.

"Oh gods!" My eyes went to the back of my head, the sensations overwhelming. Her sweet, wet tongue delving into my most neglected erogenous zone, combined with the tight heat gripping my shaft, had me about to explode. "I can't hold back any longer, Kaia."

"Then don't," she moaned, licking into another kyuban.

Tingokku! "I want you to climax first," I growled.

"Yes. I'm ready. So ready." And with one more grind on my cock, she cried out.

"Ty. Oh *Tyyyy!*" Her entire body convulsed, the spasms around my cock setting me off.

"Kaia..." I clamped my hand down on the back of her neck and kissed her collarbone, my body on fire. I pumped hot seiki into her body—groaning, grunting, riding the waves of pleasure along with her till we were both spent.

I laid down on the couch, gathering her on top of me, both of us panting and shaking.

Heated, whispered words poured from my lips about her

magnificence, her perfection. How utterly beautiful she was as I stroked her back.

My mate.

My destiny.

Mine.

9

KAIA

I WOKE to a loud banging on the door.

"Kaia! Open up. I need to talk to you!"

Crap. I'd know that voice anywhere.

What was he doing here?

Ty had already woken up, rolling me underneath him, coiling his tentacles around me protectively. "Who is that?" he whispered urgently.

"Makaio."

Ty's features pinched in obvious anger. "Why would he come here?"

"I don't know."

Makaio pounded again. "Kaia, it's about your mom."

My mom? I went to get up, sliding out from under Ty.

"What are you doing?" he asked.

"I have to see what's wrong." Sure, my mom and I weren't really on speaking terms, but I didn't wish her any ill will. If I could help, I would.

He sighed. "I think this is a bad idea."

Maybe, but I had to check. I jumped up and quickly pulled on my shorts and my shirt. "Get down so he doesn't see you."

"Hold on," I yelled, and waited as Ty reluctantly lay down out of sight.

I unlocked the door and swung it open.

"Hey, baby," Makaio said. Then he lunged for me.

I wasn't fast enough to escape and screamed as he grabbed me. He pushed me inside the house and covered my mouth.

Ty sat up from the couch, his lower half still out of sight. Makaio stopped. "Who the fuck are you?"

"Let her go and I won't kill you," Ty said, glaring at Makaio.

Makaio laughed, his hand slipping from my mouth. "What's he trying to say? What *language* is that? Shit, you really are a pilialoha."

"I am not a slut." I kicked my good leg back, catching him in the nuts.

"Ilio wahine!" he croaked, letting go of me.

"And a proud bitch at that, asshole," I retorted.

"That's it," Ty said, crawling over the couch, flinging a tentacle at Makaio in a rage.

Makaio's eyes went wide as Ty moved me aside and rushed at him.

"What are you?" Makaio spat out as Ty dragged him out of the house, a tentacle wrapped around his neck, and into the front yard. Makaio tried to scream, clawing at the thick tentacle tightening around his throat.

Another tentacle coiled around his ankle and swiftly had him hanging upside-down in the gray morning light. Ty proceeded to punch, slap, and fling Makaio about like a boxer's bag—his muscles ignited by fury. "You deserve to suffer for what you did."

With the tentacle around his neck released, Makaio screamed.

"Ty, please stop. People will hear."

Ty didn't seem to care. His gaze was focused squarely on one man, batting him around like a toy.

"Ty! *Please*!" I shouted, and he turned to see me.

He nodded and stopped, reluctantly setting Makaio down. "He doesn't deserve your mercy."

Makaio was cursing and wiping blood from his nose as he scrambled to his feet and stumbled to his truck. His eyes were wide and his hands shook as he struggled to open the door and get in.

"No, but he's not worth your trouble." I said, as the asshole peeled away in a cloud of dust, gone with a squeal of tires.

"Did he hurt you? Are you okay?" Ty checked me all over as soon as Makaio was out of sight.

"I'm fine. He just startled me, is all."

"That kick was amazing. It seems you're a better warrior than me." He winked.

I laughed, shaking my head. But I found I stood a few inches taller at his compliment. My dad would've been proud, too. I gazed out toward the street, the sun breaking through the gray clouds. "We need to go. He'll be back with his friends for sure. He hates to lose."

Ty crossed his arms and sat on the porch steps. "Let him return. I may not be the best warrior, but I'm sure I could take on all of them with ease."

"And I don't doubt it, but here on Earth we have weapons."

"Weapons? I have no problem with spears, arrows, and clubs."

I leaned against a splintered post. "He wouldn't be using those, Ty. He's got a gun."

He gave me a confused look. I had a feeling they didn't have guns on Co'sentyx.

"You can't outrun or deflect a bullet with your tentacles," I said gently.

"Fine," he grunted. "I trust you know more about your world than me."

"Thank you. Plus, we aren't allowed to kill people on Earth just for being assholes, you know."

Ty looked scandalized. "Even if he attacked you?"

I peeled some paint from the railing. "It's...complicated."

"Earth astounds me."

"Agreed," I huffed. "And I'm worried now. Makaio's pride was wounded, so he'll want revenge. And now that he's seen you, he can give away your location."

Ty regarded me with that silvery gaze, and I took a deep breath.

"We need to find that portal. Now."

10

TY'ZIR

Kaia hobbled back into the house.

"Okay, but I'm not going anywhere without you," I replied. "Especially not with that cretin after you."

She came out again with a set of keys jangling in her hand, and my satchel. She tossed the bag at me as she opened the door to the truck, then pointed to the truck bed. "Get in."

Oh no, not this again.

I crawled in, bracing myself.

She started the truck and took off, speeding down the black-colored path.

I will not vomit.

I will not vomit.

As we careened our way down the mountain toward the beach, I focused on Makaio and how much I wanted him dead. How dare he come after Kaia, after everything he'd already put her through?!

"You okay back there?" Kaia asked through the back window.

"Yes," I lied through gritted teeth. By all the gods, it would be the only time I lied to her for the rest of my life.

We made it to the beach, and Kaia got out of the truck and grabbed my hand, her eyes boring into mine. "I'm going back to Co'sentyx with you."

I blinked, ready to let out a cheer.

Then my stomach heaved.

I vomited over the side of the truck bed next to her.

"That wasn't exactly the reaction I was expecting."

"Me either," I said, wiping my mouth, then gathering her into my arms and kissing the top of her head. "Forgive me if I don't kiss your beautiful mouth at the moment."

"You're forgiven," she said with a grin, her arms around me.

I savored the moment. "Then you truly believe we're mates?"

"Of course! How else could the thought of not having you next to me fill me with a sadness even greater than the loneliness already there? I've only known you for a day and yet it feels like a lifetime."

I couldn't help but beam. "And you'll be okay leaving Earth behind?"

"As long as there are beaches to surf and strong coffee to drink, I'll be fine. My mother wrote me off long ago, and I'd prefer never to lay eyes on Makaio and his crew ever again. There's really nothing holding me here besides memories. And those are all in here." She tapped her head.

Suddenly, a familiar vehicle squealed into the lot. "Speaking of Makaio," I snarled.

"Shit!" she spat. "I thought he would go back to my place, but he must've noticed my truck here."

I tugged on her arm. "You need to go first, Kaia. Get back out to sea. Hopefully, you'll stumble on the portal again. Just believe that. Will you?"

She looked at me with frantic eyes. "What if I don't find it? What if you don't find it after me?"

"What other choice do we have? It's a risk we'll have to take. We'll face whatever comes together." I held her chin in my fingers. "We're mates. That's how it works."

She gave me a tentative smile, and I grabbed her board from the truck. "Now go!"

She took the board from me, still looking unsure. Then she pressed a huge kiss to my cheek. "See you soon, my mate."

I winked. "You'd better believe it."

"Be careful." She squeezed my hand for a second, holding my gaze. Then she was gone, taking off down the shore, kicking up sand in her wake.

I would see her in Co'sentyx. The fates had decided.

I cracked my knuckles and stretched my tentacles, ready to put these pathetic human men in their place.

Watch out, Makaio. You messed with the wrong Kisq'ali.

11

KAIA

IGNORING the tightness in my chest and the angry shouts and yells coming from the parking lot, I made it into the water.

I was worried sick about Ty, but I needed to trust him.

Paddling out as quickly as I could to the spot where I had been yesterday morning, the bracing spray of the waves had me laser focused. I dove under as the waves crashed all around me, my wet clothes pulling at me. When I felt as if I was far enough out, I sat on my board and faced the shore.

A couple of men were face down on the beach. Oh my God, had Ty actually killed them?

I couldn't think about that now. All that mattered was that he was heading for the water. To me!

I went to grab the necklace my father had given me, but it wasn't there. It must've fallen off at some point. No!

Looking up to heaven, I closed my eyes.

Help me find this portal, Dad. I'm not leaving you, I'm just changing beaches. Like you did. You'll always be with me.

The swell surged behind me. Keeping my eyes firmly on Ty as he hit the water, I lifted up my chest on my board. With a busted ankle, there would be no way to stand. Bodyboarding would have to be good enough. I leaned into the wave and caught it, riding the best I could.

A gunshot rang out.

Ty!

The distraction made me slip up and before I knew it the sea had flipped me over and I had gone under. I opened my eyes to see the ocean floor, the movement of the water, and the waves pummeling me from above. Only vast emptiness echoed around me.

Breaching the surface, I found my board and looked out toward the shore.

Immediately, I knew I was somewhere else.

The water was a vivid cobalt blue—clear and clean—and the sand a brilliant white. There was no parking lot to be seen, or cars or buildings lining the shore, only a myriad of rich green foliage and flowers, the rocks shining silvery gray.

Holy shit! I'd gone through the portal!

But where was Ty? Did he make it? Was he just behind me?

I began paddling for shore. "Ty!" I called out as I made my way to the sand.

Dropping my board, I turned to scan the ocean under the crystal-clear sky, avoiding looking at the low-hanging sun, which was so bright it was painful to look at it directly.

"*Ty!*" I yelled again.

He should have made it through by now, right?

I sat down on the sand, my eyes squinting hard against the brightness of this world for what seemed like ages, desperately searching among the waves.

Where was he? The last thing I'd heard was that gunshot. Did he...?

No, I couldn't believe that. Not after everything we'd been through.

Time passed, and the waves lapped up on the shore, not bringing anything in with them. My eyes misted.

What had I done? Now I was here alone in a strange world. Without Ty. Without my mate.

My heart twisted in my chest, and I put my face in my hands and wept.

"Why are you crying, my beautiful mate?" came a raspy, recognizable voice.

My heart leaped. I looked up to see Ty emerging from the water, his tentacles rolling up and over the wet sand.

I scrambled over to tackle him before he could make it much further, kissing him all over his sexy face.

"You're here. You're here. You're here," I kept whispering in between kisses.

Ty held me and spun me around in his arms. "And you're here with me! I am complete."

He shifted me in his arms and began carrying me down the beach.

"Are you hurt? I heard a gunshot," I said worriedly, clutching at him.

He smirked. "Barely a scratch. Out of the six 'friends' Makaio brought with him, three ran off the second they saw me. Then two more took off after I started attacking them."

I swallowed, not sure if I wanted to know. "Did you kill them? I thought I saw..."

"I did not. Though Makaio deserved it," he said, his expression dark. "I knocked them unconscious and headed straight for the water. I guess Makaio went back to his truck and grabbed a weapon..."

His shotgun.

"But it was too late. I had already gone into the water."

I hugged him even tighter, inhaling his salty musk. "You're incredible."

"There are those, like Ax'ryon, who would say that is debatable," he replied, winking. "Are you okay?"

I nodded. "I am now that you're here. I'm just a little bummed I lost the necklace my dad gave me."

He furrowed his brow, then opened his satchel and reached inside it. "This necklace, by chance?" he asked, putting something in my hand.

I recognized the black kukui nuts and white shells immediately.

"Oh! Yes! Wherever did you find it?" I gasped.

He smiled. "On the rocks, right before I first saw you out on the waves."

"Woah." I don't know what that was about, but I was glad to have it back.

"Welcome to Co'sentyx, my mate."

I grinned. "It's beautiful, just like you said."

He squeezed me.

"But I could really use some coffee. Since we were so rudely awakened this morning, I didn't get my fix. I'm fading fast."

He squinted uncomfortably. "About that... We, um, don't have coffee here."

I glared at him. "*What*?"

He hurried on. "Please don't be mad. I didn't want you to change your mind about coming."

I blinked and took a moment to grieve. No coffee. Ever again.

But on the other hand, a man who risked his life, crossing from another world to love and protect me.

What do you think, Dad?

My necklace seemed to glow in my hand, and I swear the tattoos on Ty's torso did too.

"I'll live." I kissed his cheek. "You're totally worth it, my mate. And who knows, maybe you have coffee beans here and have just never tried sticking 'em in hot water."

I mean, if there's one thing I've learned from all of this...

Anything's possible.

REBEL
MINE

INTERSTELLAR PORTALS BOOK 3

JINX LAYNE

1

SHAWNA

REST IN POWER, Leah.

I waded in until the warm blue-green waves were up to my waist and huffed out a sob.

This beach was roughly a mile away from where my best friend had fallen to her death.

Tragic.

And *all* my fault.

Why did I have to convince Leah to go on that hike? The one I'd read about in *Shape* magazine, that included scaling the side of a mountain off the coast of Kaua`i?

She'd never done any hiking before. Sure, she was independent and well-traveled, but the last thing I should've done to help her get over that scumbag, Darren, was to suggest she try something so dangerous as the Kalalau Trail.

How could I have been so dumb?

It probably had something to do with the asshole I was stuck with at home. Maybe I felt the need to live vicariously through Leah because *my man* barely looked my way, despite having plenty of opinions of how I should live my life.

I should've gone with you, girl. I'm so sorry.

Above me, I noticed storm clouds had appeared overhead. Crap, when had those moved in?

I turned to look back at the shore. Wow. Somehow I had gotten much further out than I had planned. The frothy waves reached my shoulders now, and the ocean swelled with the rough tide.

The sky and the water had both turned from a clear blue to a dark gray.

What was going on?

Suddenly, my feet were swept out from under me, and the sea pulled me out even further. Barely keeping my head up, my eyes widened in fear as I saw the huge wall of water right in front of me, the size of a house.

I'm fucked.

My whole body ached.

I opened my eyes, then covered them quickly. Oh my God, that's bright!

I felt sand under me. Dry sand.

I remembered the ocean tossing me around before I ducked under that massive wave.

Then nothing.

Could that wave have carried me back to the shore?

I carefully pushed myself up to a sitting position—

Ouuchh!

Sand was everywhere, and I mean everywhere, inside and out of my bikini.

I checked myself over for bumps, bruises, and scratches, amazed at the lack of visible injuries on my body given how sore I felt. That monster of a wave had to have tossed me around like a ragdoll. How I hadn't drowned in the process was a mystery.

"You're one lucky bitch, Shawna," I said aloud. My eyes had adjusted by now and I looked in front of me.

Everything was...different.

I spun around and looked along the shoreline behind me.

Besides the sparkling sand, intense colors of the plants and trees, and the pink flowers in the distance...there was absolutely no sign of people.

I could swear there had been buildings off to my right before. And signs warning me not to litter or trespass. *Yeah, yeah. I know.*

But I didn't see those now.

Was this a different beach entirely? Could I really have been washed out that far?

I stood up and brushed myself off. Even the sand felt... softer. Still super uncomfortable when wet and in every crevice of my body, but at least it felt nice under my bare feet.

I walked toward the forest—more of a jungle, really—in front of me.

When I reached the hot pink flowers, they were so vibrant, with soft and velvety petals, and long yellow stamen jutting out from the center, that I had to touch them. I'd never seen such big, beautiful flowers in my life.

Birds chirped loudly in the tree canopy above; their songs were also unfamiliar. I couldn't place them.

Walking further into the forest, things got even weirder, from the unusual bark on the tall trees to the strange designs on the neon green leaves of the lush plants sprouting up in between. There was an obvious shimmer to them.

Was this some kind of special habitat? A nature preserve?

Thick vines ran along the forest floor, and I picked my way carefully over them as I walked through, gaping at all the fascinating foliage.

I sat down on one of the larger vines to study a mushroom

that could've popped right out of *Alice in Wonderland*. It was such a crazy mix of neon colors and wild shapes, I almost expected to see a caterpillar smoking a hookah nearby.

I was just reaching up to touch the dazzling cap when the vine under my ass began to slide.

I yelped, jumping to my feet in an instant. Then all the vines began to shift, encircling my arms, my legs, and waist before I could think about getting away.

What the...?

"Hey!" I jerked and thrashed about, trying to get free. But it was no use. These things were sturdy.

Then came the laughter.

Deep, male laughter.

My eyes went wide as four...I couldn't tell what they were...emerged from the forest as if they were part of it.

Their shape was humanoid, with heavily muscled limbs, but their skin looked textured and...green. *Huh.* Leaves were draped around their bodies in a way that reminded me of long hair on thin vines, but it wasn't their hair. For that, they had varying lengths of twine about their heads, similar to dreadlocks and also very green. Flowers sprouted from the twine, on some of the creatures more than others, and in different colors.

They were completely naked except for a large leaf—ooh, how convenient—that covered and cradled their junk like a sling.

One of the guys, larger and thicker than the others, had variegated red flowers atop his head and when he leered at me, I saw that his eyes were the same mottled red.

Woah. Who *were* these guys?

They talked and cheered in a language I couldn't understand. I'd never heard anything like it.

One of them approached me as he spoke, his lip curled up

in a sneer. He had orange flowers in his hair that matched his eyes.

When he reached out to touch me, I jerked back. "Think again, asshat!" I yelled.

They all just laughed, and the one with orange flowers turned away.

That's when I saw the vines sprouting from his back. I followed their twists and turns, realizing he was the one holding my arms.

Then I followed the vines around my legs to find that each one led to a different dude, and the vines around my waist were emerging from the biggest guy, the one with red flowers.

Shit.

And they were all looking at me as if I was the main course at dinner.

2

GAR'EK

"I think I deserve a whole burak for dinner tonight, boss," Jik'tar said, licking his lips as he walked with me toward the main hold. "Wait till you see what we got you."

The men had said they had a 'special surprise' for me.

But I'd learned not to get my hopes up. Last time, I had returned from my rounds to find an empty cell. Ax'ryon, the leader of the Rex'ulti clan, had escaped with the help of his human mate, Lee'yah.

And Lee'yah had knocked Jik'tar out.

"You dare to make such demands when you can be incapacitated by a rock thrown by a female?"

Jik'tar grumbled.

When I arrived at the cell, I saw a figure within it.

"No, really, we got one, Gar'ek!" Fo'piz cheered. "A human woman!"

My vines bristled at his words.

Could it be true?

I strode over to the thick twine bars of the cell and stared.

She was leaning back against the wall, seated on the stone bench, her eyes closed.

She was magnificent.

The other two human women that had already come through the portal were beautiful enough, but this one...

Perfection.

Smooth, dark skin, firm muscles, lush lips, and a bounty of black hair that rose from her head like smoke from a glorious bonfire.

Saliva actually dripped from my mouth, and I quickly wiped it away.

Her eyes fluttered open, and that's when I nearly choked and had to wrap my hands around the twine bars for balance.

The were like the brilliant colors of the sky as the sun lowered over the Hexzif Forest.

She gasped and backed up against the wall when she saw me, drawing her legs up under her. She only wore a few scraps of garments, leaving her dewy skin exposed.

I saw her tremble.

"She's cold, you scum!" I barked at my men. "Why haven't you given her a fur?!"

Fo'piz shrugged. "We've never done anything like that for prisoners befo—"

"Get one *now*!" I roared, and the men scattered to do my bidding.

My hands tightened on the bars, unable to tear my gaze away from her.

Something stirred deep in my gut, making my cock thicken. My heart was pounding so hard I thought I might be ill.

What was wrong with me?

I gulped. It couldn't be...

My mate.

No. I didn't believe in that burak nonsense.

I had lived for nearly thirty star cycles. I never went near the Cave on Unmei to receive my "destiny".

I made my *own* destiny.

And my destiny had nothing to do with mating.

The woman rubbed her arms, but couldn't look away from me either.

"Whydontyoutakeapictureitlllastlongerjerkwad?" she said, in a tone that was pure attitude. I couldn't understand her words, but reading her body language was easy enough.

My cock hardened. I liked feisty women.

"Wowcallingyounamesturnsyouon? Fuckingpsycho," she continued.

I would have told her to shut her mouth, but I was enjoying watching her lips move too much.

"I got the fur," Jik'tar said, as he went to open the cell.

I wrenched the garment from his grip and roughly pushed him out of the way.

"Leave."

He looked down at my bulge, and chuckled. "You going to take her, then?" he asked. "Can I have a turn after?"

White-hot anger sliced through me at the thought of Jik'-tar's disgusting hands touching her. My vines whipped out with a snap and grabbed him by the neck, lifting him clear off the ground. "Touch her and you die," I snarled.

He gasped for air, choking and wriggling, his vines flailing about. If he used them on me, he'd suffer the consequences.

The other men watched in horror until I finally dropped him. He curled up and clutched at his neck, wheezing.

"See to him," I said to Pa'kol and Fo'piz. "The woman will stay in my quarters. Do *not* disturb us."

3

SHAWNA

ALL I COULD DO WAS SCREAM when the towering violet-eyed plant guy with the crazy big muscles barged into the cell.

I'd seen what he'd done to the big red-eyed guy.

He'd laid that boy *out*.

Although, from the body language, I was pretty sure it was...over me? Interesting.

When I first saw Violet Eyes outside the cell, something happened. It's like I knew him. Or...felt him...or... Shit, I'm not making any sense.

All I know is that my heart raced, my stomach fluttered, and my pussy—she *clenched*.

Which is ridiculous because —*hello*— he's a plant man!

Now, he made a beeline for me, and without a word lifted me up. Ignoring my pounding and kicking and flailing, he tossed me over his shoulder and held me tight against him like I was a tiny child. He didn't even have to use his vines. I kept wriggling and smacking at him, but he didn't bat an eye as he hauled me out of the cell.

Eventually, I got tired of my futile efforts and just hung

there limply as he made his way through the forest until he got to a small cluster of homes. It kind of reminded me of the Ewok village from *Star Wars*. We passed other plant people—men, women, and children—who all stopped to look at us curiously.

Whenever I cried out for help along the way, his vines would slap my hand. Not hard, but enough to get his message across. Hmph.

The homes around us were knotted twine huts set back among the trees. We went higher, and he climbed some wide stairs that led into a gargantuan hollowed-out tree.

We went through a series of rooms until he set me down. Finally!

No. My freedom was short-lived: he had me tied up in his vines again in mere seconds.

I mean, it wasn't horrible.

He moved in closer, looming over me, and I tilted my head back to meet his gaze.

I wouldn't let him scare me.

Although, to be honest, something told me I didn't need to be afraid of him.

His eyes were stunning. Like the inside of quartz rock, deep with intricate facets and shades of color, and thin pupils that reminded me of a cat's. Just like the other plant guys, the flowers tucked into his twine hair were the same violet as his eyes.

I desperately wanted to reach out and touch the flower at his temple, to feel the texture.

"Yakim mekina bae hajin," he said, his eyes roving over my face. His voice was low and raspy, and it sent shivers down my spine.

He arranged the fur blanket over my shoulders and walked into the other room, while the vines stayed put around me.

I shook my head in disbelief.

Where the hell was I? Who were these creatures?

And most importantly—I had a sudden thought—could Leah be here?

They'd never found her body. We assumed it had disintegrated to nothing in the fall, but the authorities said it was highly unusual not to have *anything* wash up on the shore, especially considering she had been wearing clothes, boots, and a small pack.

Maybe she did end up here.

...Wherever *here* was.

Violet Eyes came back into the room carrying a bowl and held up a bluish-red berry.

"Miko bahei," he said, pressing it to my lips. I figured it would be okay to eat and opened my mouth. As I chewed, bright, sweet juice filled my mouth. It had flesh like a blueberry, but more of the flavor of a mango.

"Grilen?" he asked, and I nodded. I wasn't sure if he was asking if I liked it or if I wanted more, but the answer to both of those was a yes.

He fed me five more of the plump berries. Whoa, I was hungrier than I thought. I guess getting swept out to see and into another world really took it out of you. He then held up something that looked like a peach. "Ghabi fokiz." He took a bite of it to show me, the juice slicking his lush lips. Then he offered it to me so that I could take a bite.

Yum. So fresh and citrusy. When the juice ran down my chin, he was right there to wipe it up with his finger. The tip of it brushed my lip, sending a jolt of pleasure through me.

He licked his finger clean while his gaze held mine.

Okay, *fuck*, that was seriously hot. Although I must be a total freakazoid to be drooling over Swamp Thing.

He let me finish the fruit, then put the bowl down.

"What is your name?" I asked.

"Naaame?" he replied, furrowing his brow.

"Name," I nodded.

"Name," he said, this time correctly.

I shoved my wrists forward. "Please," I said. I'd need my hands to help pantomime what I was saying to him, and it did look like he wanted to help me.

Just when I was convinced he'd decided against it, the vines on my wrists slid off.

"Thank you," I said, rubbing the skin on my arms.

"Name," he repeated again, but I doubted he understood exactly what it meant.

I put my palms to my chest. "Shaw-na," I said, sounding it out for him carefully. "Shaw-na."

"Shah-nah," he replied slowly in that deep, gravelly voice that felt like fingernails dancing down my back.

Normally I *hated* when people got that wrong, but today? Close enough.

I nodded enthusiastically. "Yes!"

Then I reached out and touched his chest. "Name?"

His eyes followed my hand on his chest. The rapid beating of his heart held my palm like a magnet.

I felt his muscles expand under my touch and my name slipped out of his mouth again in a growly whisper.

Fuck. He needed to stop that, like, yesterday. My swimsuit bottoms were getting wetter by the moment.

His eyes closed and he inhaled deeply. The vines around my legs began to slide, much too sensuously.

I cleared my throat. "Name," I said again firmly, tapping his hard chest. His eyes flew open.

We both seemed to be getting distracted.

"Gar'ek," he finally said.

"Gar'ek," I repeated, nodding. I swear his body trembled, and the vines tightened again on my legs.

He turned abruptly as if in pain and went to sit down on what looked to be a bed in the center of the room, covered in furs.

"Gar'ek?" I asked. But he just threw up his palm in a "stop" gesture...or at least that's how I interpreted it...and then rubbed his hand over his chiseled jawline.

Our language lesson was over, apparently.

I tried to move under the weight of his vines. Was it tiring for him, having to be attached to me at all times?

The sun was beginning to set, and shadows had started filtering into the room as I surveyed the space.

It had other furniture—chairs, small tables, and interesting knick-knacks that I would have loved to ask about. It was all very primitive. I didn't see any sort of modern technology, like phones or computers, TVs or even artificial lights.

I yawned. The long day was beginning to wear on me.

He noticed and got up, the vines sliding over my legs, encouraging me to walk toward him.

I knew he wouldn't hurt me, but I really wasn't sure what he wanted.

"Sha'nah," he said, patting the bed. "Sevinjik."

Oh god. Did he want sex?

And why did my pussy clench...*again*?

No. I had to get a hold of myself and ignore my insane attraction to this guy...plant...dude. And I needed to keep my wits about me if I was to find Leah (if she was even around) and get out of here.

He took my hand and pulled me down onto the bed next to him, the vines releasing to allow me to lie down. I wanted to ask about Leah, but as my head hit the soft fur on the bed, sleep called to me and my eyes drifted shut.

His vines slid over me as he tucked the fur blanket over my shoulders.

The last thing I remembered was his big warm body settling in behind mine.

4

GAR'EK

I WATCHED Sha'nah sleeping in my bed, her beautiful body a mere breath away.

It was pure torture to stop my vines from exploring her and pleasuring her. I longed to coax sweet sounds from her pretty throat, to make her cry out in orgasm—

Stop, Gar'ek. You'll wake her.

I couldn't do any of those things.

She was my captive to be used as leverage to help me take back power for the Sun'ozi. Nothing more.

No matter how much my body ached for her.

I forced myself to move as far away from her as possible on my bed, but she only backed that plump, juicy ass closer to me.

My cock raged.

I thought about pleasuring myself to take the edge off, but I didn't think it would make much of a difference, not even if I spent myself twenty times over.

I could easily resist the women in my clan.

With Sha'nah, I could barely remember my name.

I was a slave to this feeling! And I hated that.

I lay there for what seemed like forever, my body tense and uneasy, until finally fatigue won out and I succumbed to sleep.

Something tickled my nose, and I opened my eyes.

A warm, thick body was nestled against me, and dark hair brushed over my face.

I groaned and inhaled her sweet, musky scent. The one that she released every time her body betrayed her need.

Sha'nah.

She clung to me, her hot breath on my neck, her body intertwined with mine, my vines wrapped around even the most intimate of places.

I dared not move.

My dreams came rushing back to me, wild and frantic and primal, of Sha'nah and I locked in an embrace. Of my vines holding her and exploring her sweet skin.

I disentangled myself as best I could and lay on my back, staring up at the thatched roof.

What was happening to me?

She stirred and stretched her arms over her head, moaning, while I pretended to be still asleep.

"Holy fuck—it wasn't a dream," she said, her voice husky as she wakened.

Gods!

I could understand her.

Could it be true? The mating bond?

How did we—

"Why do I find you so... irresistible?" she whispered, next to my shoulder. "I wish you could tell me."

I knew she thought I was asleep.

Could we perhaps have performed the bonding rite in our sleep?

Her fingers traveled lazily over my chest and I struggled to keep my body in check. When she grazed my nipple, I bit back a moan.

I suppose it *was* possible that our foreheads had touched in the night cycle and we had cupped each other's faces to perform the rite.

Incredible.

Her hands traveled further down, leaving a searing hot trail to my groin.

"Wow," she whispered. "You need a bigger leaf to hide that bad boy."

She reached out for the sepal that covered my cock, and I clasped her wrist.

"No, my Sha'nah," I warned.

She jumped, and the bed creaked beneath us.

"Hey now! How long have you been awake?" She cocked her head, her eyes wide.

"You were going to peek at my cock while I was asleep." I shook my head and tsked at her.

Her cheeks flushed.

So lovely.

"I was just— Wait! Why can I understand you now? You're speaking English."

I sat up, pulling her with me. "No, I'm not speaking your language. You are just now able to understand mine, when I speak it. It is called Co'senti. It is the language of the clans here on this planet."

"P-planet?" She swallowed hard and stared at me. "I'm on another planet?"

I nodded.

She pulled out of my grasp and wrapped her arms around

herself, shaking her head. "Stop for a moment. I'm trying to think." Her eyes darted all around.

"I wasn't able to understand you earlier. And you couldn't understand me." I flicked my gaze between her and the bed again. "And then we bonded."

She drew back and blinked. "Excuse me? We did *what* now?"

"Bonded," I repeated, almost smiling at her adorably puzzled expression. "We must have done it as we slept."

Her brow furrowed. "Are you saying you and I... hooked up?"

"I don't know that I would call it "hooked up". Sun'ozi don't have hooks. We have vines." I lifted one of my vines to show her.

"Funny. You're funny." She leveled her gaze at me. "Hooked up means"...she bit her lip..."have sex."

"No!" I huffed, appalled. "Not mere sex. Bonding is a rite performed by two mates."

"Mates?" she said. "Are you kidding me?"

"If two mates bond, the connection reveals what needs to be known. Including language."

She put her head in her hand. "I'm so confused."

"As am I."

"Why are you confused? This is *your* planet. *Your* way of life."

I shrugged. "I've never believed in this fated mate muck."

She looked up at me and smiled. "Thank God. Because I sure as hell don't."

5

SHAWNA

I WAS SHOWERING in the water closet of a big tree house *on a different planet*. I never thought I'd form that sentence in my head.

There had to be a reasonable explanation for all this. Beyond "fated mates", that is.

I groaned. Such bull.

That said... It *would* explain a lot.

As the warm water fell from large wooden pipes above— reminiscent of the *Swiss Family Robinson*—I remembered how wonderful it had been to be wrapped in Gar'ek's vines, lost in his violet eyes, and touched by his textured skin.

It's like my body craved it. I was hungrier for him than the miko berries and ghabi fruit he gave me again this morning. And those were *delicious*.

Did he emit some kind of pheromones or something? Aphrodisiac pollen? Sexy chlorophyll?

I didn't get it.

I'd convinced him to let me shower without the vines, promising I wouldn't try to run or escape. Though now I almost missed the vines around me. I imagined them sliding back and forth over my wet pussy, making me come in an instant.

God, I really was addicted. *And kinky.*

I needed to focus. He was my only hope of finding Leah and getting home.

I dressed in the fur-hide top and skirt he gave me. I looked like I was going to a Halloween party as a sexy cavewoman. I fluffed up my afro and found Gar'ek in a room with shelves filled with books. He was flipping through a large, old volume, his fine bare backside on display. Dayum, he was ripped *everywhere.*

"What are you doing?" I asked, my voice hoarse, and he turned around, still holding the book in his arms. He looked me up and down, and I immediately felt the slick between my legs.

His bulge was already thick behind that poor leaf straining at his groin.

"I'm searching my father's ancient texts for any mention of the portal and the visitors."

I blinked. "You think this whole portal to other planets business is a real thing?"

"If you believe the ancient texts. They were written by a group of beings that no longer live here. Supposedly they established settlements on the planet Co'sentyx and brought each clan here through the portal."

"That's wild." I sat down in one of the chairs near him.

"Throughout the history of Co'sentyx there have been stories of visitors from other planets. But it's difficult to pinpoint exactly how or why they came. Most of the beings on Co'sentyx believe in fate. They can't comprehend a world full of randomness. I, on the other hand, think we cannot possibly know all that goes on in the universe. In other words, I say sometimes there are accidents."

"Preaching to the choir, my friend," I said, nodding.

He cocked his head to the side. "I don't understand."

"It means, you're telling someone who already agrees with you."

A small smile spread over his lips. That was a first. It was soft and special, and my stomach churned in response.

"Have you had any recent visitors?" I asked.

He squinted down at me, as if weighing the pros and cons of telling me the truth. I felt it in my bones. It seemed much easier to read him after last night. Gosh, maybe we really had bonded, as he called it.

"Two," he finally said, setting the book on the table heavily.

"Two? Really?" I reached out to take his hand. He seemed taken aback. "Humans?"

His eyes darted from our hands to my face and then away again. Something was bothering him.

"Tell me, Gar'ek," I said, my voice an intense whisper.

"You do not issue the demands, Sha'nah," he said, pulling out of my grasp. "I am the leader of the Sun'ozi, soon to be leader of all Co'sentyx."

Stubborn, megalomaniac alien ass.

I continued to look up at him, waiting. Two could play that game.

"Yes," he finally mumbled. "One woman came to us over a star cycle ago. The other one, just under half a star cycle. Both human."

Oh my God...

"On my planet, Earth, I'd gone to the place where my best friend had supposedly died, falling from the side of a cliff into the ocean. Her body has never been found. I swam into the ocean and was swept out to sea. That's how I ended up here. Is..." I was almost afraid to ask. "Is one of the women named Leah?"

His face gave it away immediately.

"She's here? Gar'ek!" I jumped up as tears spilled down my cheeks. "You have to take me to her."

Leah was alive! Jesus.

"No, not yet." He pulled from my grasp and strode away from me. "There are plans to be made and men to assemble."

"What are you talking about?"

"Lee'yah is mated to Ax'ryon, the leader of the Rex'ulti, our rival clan. They rule Co'sentyx with their allies, the Kisq'ali. Kaia, the other human woman, is mated to Ty'zir, the leader of that clan."

Holy shit. Leah got herself a warrior alien? Take that, Darren.

"Wait... What do you mean by rival clan?" I asked nervously.

"The Rex'ulti, and their allies the Kisq'ali, are sworn enemies of the Sun'ozi. They'd kill us if we got anywhere near them."

"Would they kill me?"

"No." He looked at me steadily. "Which is why the Sun'ozi need you to breach their villages."

Not what I expected *at all*.

"So... I'm just a pawn in all of this?" I scrubbed my face and turned to go.

Anywhere but here.

Gar'ek caught up to me and grabbed my wrist, wrapping his vines around my legs to stop me. This again? "Dude, you can't just use force any time you feel like it."

"I can and I will, Sha'nah. I've given you too much free rein already."

I narrowed my eyes at him. "You know what? You're a brute, Gar'ek. A big ol' bully."

His violet eyes flashed like a bolt of lightning had hit them and he wrapped his big hand around my neck.

"I am no such thing, woman," he growled.

I knew I should be afraid, but I held his fiery gaze.

"Listen to me," he said. "My father spent his entire *life* trying to take back the power the Rex'ulti and Kisq'ali stole from us. I watched how it ruined him. Watched how they continually defeated us in battle, until we had no choice but to crawl away to tend to our wounds."

He turned to gaze out the window. "But there had been a drought. And we were low on the biostyk we use to make our healing poultices. Most of our warriors died, since the only other medicine on our planet is behind enemy lines. The evoki plant only grows near the Kisq'ali caves and the Rex'ulti village. They wouldn't allow us to gather any for our sick and injured."

He ground his jaw. "My father died from a Rex'ulti spear wound that became infected. On his deathbed I vowed to bring the pure land dwellers back to rule Co'sentyx. And I'm going to fulfill that promise no matter what."

A single sparkly tear fell down his cheek.

"I'm sorry..." I whispered as his forehead bowed to rest on mine. "I'm so sorry."

His sorrow surged through me in an overwhelming wave, and my only thought was to take it away. My heart ached for him. *Everything* ached for him.

His grip on my wrist went slack, and I slid my palm to his face.

I needed to relieve his pain, if only for a short while.

I pulled his mouth down to mine and our lips met in another explosion of pure pleasure.

I whimpered as my knees buckled, but he held me firmly.

"Mine," he growled, so deep it barely registered as a word.

No argument here.

Our mouths clashed, as if fighting for dominance. I was

desperate for his heat, his taste, the newness of his rough, wet tongue.

He held my face in his hands, and we swallowed each other's moans.

He dropped to my neck, nipping and kissing and biting his way over my skin.

My hands slipped down his chiseled chest and stomach, exploring the grooves of his Adonis belt. I ran my fingers over the sharp creases of that decadent V at his groin and groaned.

He rocked forward, and suddenly his vines were all over me.

"Need you bare," he snarled against my shoulder. One vine lifted up my top, and I raised my hands so he could pull it off. Another untied the skirt from my hips and flung it aside.

He lifted my ass in his big hands and I wrapped my legs around his waist, moaning as I felt his cock grinding against my pussy.

Grunting, he carried me over to the bed and laid me down. As he crawled on top of me, his vines slithered over my naked body, probing my curves.

I cried out when he found a nipple, sucking on it, his rough tongue sending shockwaves straight to my pussy as he worked the strong ridges on the tip of his tongue around the sensitive peak.

My hands grabbed at his head, his twine hair, his vines. He shuddered when I squeezed the appendages and ran my nails over his thick green skin.

"Sha'...nah," he groaned, tugging his vines under me.

"You like that?" I whispered, running one of his leaves between my fingers. He shivered.

"Yes. As much as I like your stiff nipples," he growled, rubbing his fingertips over them. I arched back, mewling and crying out as he kissed down my stomach.

I could have come just from the way his vines slid over my

thighs and pussy. I was teetering on the edge already. The man had serious moves.

But when his mouth touched my aching mound, I moaned as if I'd never been touched there before.

"Let me taste your sweetness," he rasped.

That rough tongue made quick work of my sensitive flesh, finding all the spots that made me tremble under his lips.

"You taste like the inside of a biostyk. Hot and sweet and sending healing to my very core."

He looked up at me with those multi-faceted eyes and my heart skipped.

"I bet you say that to all your women."

His lip curled up at the side. "There are no other women. You are my shining star. The fates be damned."

He went back to my pussy, keeping his eyes on mine as his tongue danced in my folds, brushing my clit.

"Fuck, Gar'ek," I groaned, as my orgasm hit me hard and fast, wracking my body.

The vines tightened around me as he continued to lick, suck, and kiss me. I writhed, pleading with him to stop... It was such sweet torture.

When he finally let up, I lay there trying to catch my breath. "I want to do that for multiple sun cycles." Then he straddled me, getting up on his knees, and I watched as his cock sprang from its leaf cover, like an animal breaking free of a trap.

"Are you ready for me?" he asked, and my mouth dropped open.

6

GAR'EK

"I ...UH..." Sha'nah audibly gulped. "That's *huge*, Gar'ek."

"I don't think I can go another moment without being inside you, Sha'nah." The words poured out of me like water from a stream in the Hexzif Forest.

I was not one to let my cock rule me, like some other of my clan, but right now, my existence would shatter if I thought I couldn't claim Sha'nah completely.

That first taste of her decadent cunt clinched it. She was mine. And I'd do *anything* to keep her.

"That's a bold statement, Gar'ek," she said, stroking my cheek.

"I know," I said with a snarl. By all the gods, why did I feel this way so quickly and deeply? I wanted to shake my fist at the fates as they taunted me.

"Let me touch you," she said. Just her words made me shudder.

"My body is yours, my ma—" I almost said it. *Mate*. No. She may be mine, but... I would not be swayed by those ludicrous myths.

She lifted up onto her elbows, her bare breasts tempting me. My cock stood high and proud at attention.

"This..." she said, reaching out to touch the weeping tip. "Is all mine?"

I shivered as her fingers closed around my shaft just below the head.

"Yes, yours..." I croaked. "How does it compare to human males?"

"I already said it was huge, didn't I?" she smiled. "*Much*, much bigger than any man I've known." She fondled me, and I cursed, fighting for self-control. "But your skin is textured, and green, and *this* is new."

She touched the slit where my stamen had begun to lift. "That's my stamen. When I ejaculate, it rises and releases my nectar into your channel."

"I see. That explains why you don't have testicles."

"Only the Rex'ulti have balls." I spat. "Fish balls."

"Fish-balls?" she giggled.

"Never mind." I shook my head. The Rex'ulti scum were the last thing I wanted to think about as I made love to Sha'nah.

She stroked my cock with that beautiful little hand of hers and I had to hold onto a wooden beam above the bed to steady myself. "Sweet gods."

"So... What does your nectar taste like, Gar'ek?"

My brow shot up.

She smiled and pushed me onto my side next to her. She leaned down and licked the tip.

I inhaled a shaky breath. "Sha'nah..."

She opened her mouth and drew me inside. Warm, wet heat enveloped me and I thrust a hand into her hair, fisting it.

There was no need to force her deeper. She was doing very well on her own.

My stamen vibrated. Gods, I wanted to spend this very instant, shooting loads of nectar down her throat.

But no, I needed to get inside her cunt before I did that.

Her silky wet tongue swirled over my tip and her cheeks hollowed out.

"Sha'nah...please!" I'd never begged in my entire life, but this woman...

Still, my pleas only seemed to embolden her. She moaned, sending dizzying sensations through me.

"Don't make me spend yet."

She slid off and whined as if I was taking away her favorite toy. She licked her lips. "Holy fuck, Gar'ek. Your nectar tastes like honeysuckle! When I was young I'd suck the insides of a honeysuckle flower to reach the sweet juice." She purred. "You're delicious."

Gods in Tingokku.

Sun'ozi females only tolerated our nectar, finding the flavor bitter. How did I get so lucky?

I growled and pushed her onto her back. I caressed her jawline as I settled my body over hers. "Next time, my...Sha'nah. Next time, you may have all my nectar in that talented mouth of yours."

My vines slid over her body, going where my arms couldn't reach. I wanted to take my time, and pleasure her properly, but my cock could not wait. It wanted release, and it was throbbing to the point of pain.

She ran her fingers over my lips. "What about pregnancy?"

I paused. "What about it?"

"We're not using any protection. You could get me pregnant."

I'd forgotten: she didn't know how we reproduced. "My nectar is not active until about four or five spends."

"What?"

"We'd need to have intercourse and I would have to ejaculate four or five times before my nectar became...viable. Meaning it can fertilize."

She blinked up at me, those deep brown eyes searching mine. "You're not just saying that so we can have unprotected sex, are you?"

I ground my hips against hers and she gasped. "I would not lie to you about such things."

"Then what are you waiting for?" she asked with a smirk.

With that I pressed the tip of my cock against her slick folds, trembling at the sensation.

"Yes," she whispered as I slowly pushed inside, each small bit stealing a breath.

"You...incredible." I mumbled, words failing me the deeper I sank into her hot cunt.

She moaned as I began to thrust. "What is making it so slick?"

"Plasia. Our natural lubricant."

"Fuck, I love this planet," she said, and I pumped harder into her, chuckling.

I pulled her legs around me and gripped her thick ass. I wanted something to hold onto as I thrust deeper.

Her head flew back and I growled, watching her perfect breasts bounce each time I plunged inside her. My vines teased her rounded, puckered peaks and she arched back, her mouth agape.

Tight and unrelenting, her grip on my cock was maddening. With each thrust I was being squeezed and rubbed thoroughly.

If she kept this up, I would soon be exploding inside her.

Sha'nah cried out louder now, spurring me on. I set her back down on the bed, my vines pressing her legs further apart. I leaned over her, pumping harder and faster.

I flicked one of my leaves back and forth over her sweet spot at the top of her cunt, knowing I was closing in on my orgasm.

"I'm coming, Gar'ek!" she yelled, and her body convulsed and clenched, shredding the last of my control.

I erupted, my stamen jutting into her hot channel to release my nectar in heavy spurts. My body shook, but I kept thrusting, riding the waves of pleasure, wanting to give her every last drop. Every last piece of me.

I lay down next to her, my face on her shoulder, stroking her body as it quaked under my hands and vines.

She cursed and gasped and mumbled under her breath, slowly coming to rest. Our breathing finally calmed, and she ran her hands over my body.

"Gar'ek. You've ruined me."

Oh! "I hurt you?" I asked, anxiously searching her eyes. "Why didn't you—"

"No." She tugged at the vine caressing her collarbone. "I mean you ruined me for any other man. That was..."

"Magical...?" I finished for her, huffing out a breath and lying back on the bed.

She chuckled and snuggled into me. "You could say *out of this world*."

I held her tight and kissed her chin. This woman was mine.

Forever.

When I woke, I knew already that she was gone.

Her comforting warmth had disappeared, and my body had ached for her in my dreams.

I jumped up. "Sha'nah?" I yelled into the room, frantically searching the house for signs of her. "Sha'nah!"

Maybe it *had* been a dream. All of it. From the men leading me to the cell, to my first glimpse of her.

Sha'nah. *My mate.*

Yes, mate.

I knew that now. Deep in my soul.

And I needed to find her.

7

SHAWNA

I FELT as if I'd been running for ages.

When I woke up in the middle of the night, I knew I had to go find Leah, but also knew that Gar'ek would never allow it. Not with this feud between the clans.

I hated deceiving him like this, but it was the only way. The man was stubborn to a fault. Hot, sexy, and a fabulous lover, mind you. But still stubborn.

So I had made my way out of the forest, avoiding the village, to look for the shore where I had washed up.

The sun hadn't yet breached the horizon, but there was enough light to see. It still would be tough to figure out which way to go, though.

I walked along the shore, then began to pick my way over some large rock formations. It was difficult to do barefoot and in a fur top and skirt.

My thoughts kept returning to Gar'ek, and our amazing lovemaking. It wasn't just sex. I knew sex. What we had done was...so much more. Could this mate bond thing be real? Had it indeed been fate that had brought me through the portal, like it had Leah and Kaia?

My body ached just thinking about him, and even more so since last night. Would he forgive me for running off like this? Because in my heart I knew I wanted him. Fate or not—the thought of not being with him made everything hurt.

Suddenly I heard voices and looked up with a start. A woman was surfing out on the waves! A human woman!

I hustled over the rocks as fast as I safely could to get closer. Then came to a halt when I saw a man... well, a man-slash-octopus...hanging off the side of a rock, cheering the woman on.

His lower half was all tentacles, his torso human. Glowing stripes covered his arms and chest, and his face was framed by long white hair. Damn... He was pretty hot.

He let out a long, loud whistle, then yelled something to the woman. As he swung his gaze around, it landed on me.

He stopped, and his mouth fell open.

I waved and he hesitantly waved back. Then he shook it off and yelled over to the woman before he dove into the water and swam toward me.

When he popped up, I only saw his upper half.

"Hello," I said with a smile.

"Yuli undoshej mekine?" he asked. I guessed the language thing only worked with the one I was bonded to. A shame.

I shook my head. "I don't understand Co'senti."

His brow furrowed. "Yuli setikez Co'senti?"

I wasn't sure if I should nod or shake my head. "Um..."

Just then, the woman swam up to the rocks and the octopus guy used his tentacles to help her up onto them. "Oh my gosh, hi!" she said to me excitedly. "I'm Kaia." She had long black hair and dark eyes, and a tanned, athletic body that seemed made for surfing.

"I'm Shawna."

"*Shawna*?!" Kaia and Octopus Guy both exclaimed together.

147

"You're here?" Kaia added.

I laughed. "So it would appear, yes."

"I'm all wet, but can I please hug you?" Kaia asked. "I feel like I know you since Leah's told me all about you."

"She's here?! Of course!" We embraced. "Am I ever glad to see you. Where is Leah? I have so much to tell her."

"I'm sure you do!" She was about to say something else when a tentacle poked her in the arm.

She looked at it and chuckled. "Oh, sorry. This is my mate, Ty'zir," Kaia said. Ty'zir rose up from below and took my hand in both of his.

"Plasir tungo molenji yuli, Sha'nah."

"He said it's a pleasure to meet you," Kaia relayed. She clapped her hands together. "Now: how long have you been here? Are you okay? Do you need help or anything else?" Kaia rattled off, looking at me. "Where did you get the clothes?"

Ty'zir murmured something to her.

"What? How would she know that?" Kaia said, her eyes wide, turning back to me. "How would you know the word Co'senti?"

I pressed my lips together and gazed out toward the sky which was getting lighter by the minute. "I'm...bonded." I cringed a little. How did I tell them I'm bonded with their enemy?

"Bonded!? My God." Kaia slapped her forehead and looked at Ty'zir. His mouth had dropped open once again. They both stared at me. "Who did you bond with, Sha'nah?"

I swallowed and fidgeted with the now-damp fur of my top. "It's, um, a long story. I just got here a day ago."

"Who did you bond with?" Kaia asked again, reaching out to hold my wrist, her expression serious.

I took a deep breath. "Gar'ek."

Before I could even finish saying his name, Ty'zir put a hand to his heart. "Nevo, Sun'ozi!" he whispered.

"Being a little overdramatic, aren't you?" I said, rolling my eyes at him. Kaia's lips twitched into a small smile.

"He's *always* a little overdramatic," she replied, and Ty'zir snorted.

"In all honesty: did Gar'ek force you?"

"No!" I said adamantly, then paused, reconsidering. "Okay... He *did* capture me. At least, his men did, and then he brought me to his house in the village. I had to escape because I had to find Leah, plus he planned to use me somehow against your clans. Maybe threaten to hurt me or something. Although I know he'd be bluffing. I know for a fact he'd never actually hurt me."

I sighed. "Crap, I can't believe I'm betraying him and telling you all this." My heart throbbed in pain. "I just really have to see Leah, and know that she's okay."

Kaia smiled. "She's more than okay. You'll see." She looked around. "We better get moving. I'm sure once Gar'ek notices you're gone, he'll be on the hunt for you."

Why did I like hearing that? Because it meant that finally I'd found a man whose world revolved around me? Maybe.

But I certainly didn't want to endanger anyone else.

Kaia and Ty'zir led me across the rocks to another beach and into a small cove as we chatted. It was early enough that most of the Rex'ulti were not yet awake.

The ones that were awake waved cheerily at Kaia and Ty'zir, but openly gaped at me. These beings were half koi fish and half human! They had striking black-rimmed eyes, shimmering scaly skin, and fins! I tried not to let myself get overwhelmed. First plant people, then a kraken guy, now fish people? If I thought about it for too long I'd drive myself crazy.

We finally reached an unusual, thatched dwelling that was

attached to a cave. Kaia jangled the shells tied to the door. Ty'zir yelled something through it.

It took a while, but finally there was grumbling as the door opened to reveal a striking koi fish man. He was tall and wide with muscles, and his scaly skin shimmered with orange and white markings. He wore a piece of animal hide that covered his groin...barely...and he held a long spear in his clawed hand.

"Wahinez me ixay, Ty'zir?!" he growled, rubbing his eyes. When he saw me, he looked to Ty'zir and Leah. They chatted back and forth for a while, until he put out his hand. "Hello Sha-nah!" he said carefully, as if he'd been practicing English. "I am Ax'ryon."

"Hi," I replied with a smile, shaking his hand and nodding. "Nice to meet you."

"Cazil inak, plasir! Cazil!" Ax'ryon motioned for us to enter, and we did so.

The hut was cute, like a coastal yurt that led into a cozy cave area. It was big enough for all of us—tentacles, tails, and all. It was homey, with shell knick-knacks and other unusual nautical items I couldn't place.

Ax'ryon rushed through another door.

"He's gone to get Leah," Kaia said. "She's going to *freak out*."

I couldn't wait.

After a minute, Ax'ryon came back out with a groggy, half-dressed Leah, who was resting a hand on her very obvious belly.

"Oh my god! You're pregnant!" I said loudly, then covered my mouth.

Leah's eyes went wide and she screamed. "*Shawna!*"

I rushed to her and I hugged her tightly, careful to avoid her baby bump. She hugged me back, laughing and crying.

Happy tears streamed down my face, too. "I'd thought you

were dead this whole time, and here you are, about to bring a new life into the world!"

We pulled back and wiped each other's faces, laughing.

"Oh please, sit down, girl!" I said, pulling her over to something that looked like a couch. "You should be resting." I eased her down with me.

"You've met my mate, Ax?" she asked, looking over at him as the group found seats around us.

I nodded. "I did. And Kaia and Ty'zir."

"So tell me...tell us...everything," she said.

I launched into my story, starting with my visit to Kaua'i and ending with being captured by the Sun'ozi, and meeting Gar'ek.

"Are you serious?" Leah asked. "Gar'ek?"

Ax jumped up, speaking a mile a minute. Ty tried to calm him down.

I nodded. "There's more... We, um, bonded."

"*What*? You bonded with *him*?" She repeated what I head said to Ax, who was now nearly tearing out all of his long, white hair. "Are you sure?"

"I'm not entirely *sure* of anything around here, but... We were sleeping together. *Just sleeping*." I shot Leah a look. "And when we woke up, we could understand each other.

"Oh god," Leah said. "This is bad. Like, super bad."

Ax just kept pacing the room.

"Hey, he's not...horrible," I said in his defense.

"Shawna, he's led battle after battle against the Rex'ulti and Kisq'ali, just like his father before him! He's *ruthless*."

I took a deep breath. "Okay, but listen. He told me the reason he wants the Rex'ulti to be in power."

"Why?" Kaia asked.

"To have control over the planet's resources."

"And?" Leah pressed. "Why is this so important to him?"

"It's about revenge for the death of his father and tons of their warriors. He told me his father and lots of their men died because the Rex'ulti and Kis'qali were hoarding all the evoki plants. They were unable to heal their injured without them."

Leah translated for Ax.

Ax scratched his jaw and had a brief conversation with Ty. Ty said something and it was Kaia's turn to offer a translation. "He said they did have a drought that year and that many of the plants died off. Maybe the Sun'ozi are telling the truth."

Ax spoke again and Leah said, "He doesn't remember any Sun'ozi asking for evoki plants for their injured. But he will ask his mother and the elders."

"I honestly think Gar'ek would be open to a truce, if evoki and biostyk were readily available to anyone who needed it," I said. "I mean, if I could convince him, wouldn't it be worth it for all the clans?"

Leah spoke to Ax and Kaia to Ty.

Ax went over to Leah and caressed her belly gently. She smiled up at him, love in her eyes. "Peace would be worth it."

Ty nodded in agreement.

Ax whispered in her ear.

"But at the moment, the guys are more worried about what Gar'ek will do when he finds you here," Leah said. "He won't like being apart from his mate. Or the idea that she's fraternizing with the enemy."

"Then I'll just have to go back." An idea suddenly took shape. "I have a plan, but it involves all of us."

Kaia and Leah translated for their men.

Kaia spoke. "If they can keep us safe, they're on board."

My mind was made up. I wanted Gar'ek as my mate. But we had to find a solution to all this fighting, or it would never work.

I needed my best friend, *and* I needed my mate.

"We got this." But my shaky voice said otherwise.

8

GAR'EK

"FLUSH HER OUT," I'd snarled, as my best warriors and I began searching for Sha'nah in Hexzif Forest. "If you find her, you tell me. No one lays a hand, or vine, on her. Is that understood?"

Where could she have gone?

And how *dare* she?

Unless those sea-dwelling bastards from the Rex'ulti and Kisq'ali clans had stolen her away. But there was no way they could get to the Sun'ozi village.

She must have gone to them to meet Lee'yah.

I cursed.

Had she planned to betray me this whole time?

My heart ached. It didn't matter if she had betrayed me or not. She was mine. And I would take back what was mine, no matter the cost.

With each call and thrash in the weeds, my rage grew.

I wanted to rip every plant out by the roots and scream to the gods.

At the edge of the forest, near the shore, a familiar scent wafted toward me on the breeze. I inhaled long and deep.

Sha'nah.

I frantically searched all around, trying to follow her sweet scent, until my heart leapt when I spotted her walking toward me from the sand.

We both stopped and stared. The big beaming smile on her face melted my heart.

She was here.

Then two other human females appeared next to her.

One was pregnant. Lee'yah.

Instantly I went on my guard. If Lee'yah and Kaia were here, that meant their mates could not be far away.

Was this a trap?

"Hold, Sun'ozi!" I called out to my men, who had begun to whisper.

I made my way forward, mind and body alert.

"Gar'ek," she said, and the sound of my name on her tongue filled me with deep happiness. "I brought Lee'yah and Kaia to meet you."

"Where are their mates?" I asked, as I reached them. My vines ached to touch Sha'nah, but I held back, fully aware I was out in the open and vulnerable to attack.

"They are close, but I made them both swear they'd keep their distance."

"You're a fool to believe either of them," I snapped.

"Say that again," she dared, her voice as sharp as my teeth. Her eyes blazed.

I crossed my arms over my chest. "They are not to be trusted. I told you this."

She reached out and grabbed my hand, and all I could do was stare, my body throbbing.

"Why did you go?" I asked. It came out more broken than I intended.

"You said I was your captive. If we are mates, I need to be

able to make my own choices, Gar'ek. Leah is my best friend. I needed to see her."

I huffed. "Well, you saw her. Now let's go."

I shook my head. "No. Not until you hear me out."

I narrowed my eyes at the three of them. "What is this about?"

Sha'nah kicked the sand about with her foot, as if steeling herself.

"The Rex'ulti and Kisq'ali want a truce."

I snorted. "Good for them. However, we seem to have different goals. I want to take over as leader of Co'sentyx."

"But why must you rule over them?" she asked.

"We've talked about this." I studied her carefully. "They can't be trusted to share the planet's resources."

Sha'nah told Lee'yah what I said. "Leah says Ax and Ty would be more than happy to allow anyone access to necessary resources on their lands, especially ones that help heal the injured or sick."

"That's not what your father did!" I yelled out loudly enough for Ax to hear, wherever he was. "How do I know you're not a two-faced liar just like him?"

Ax stepped out from where he had been hiding behind a rock. "I'm not my father, Gar'ek. And I am truly sorry for what he did. My mother never told me that my father denied yours evoki plants to heal his injuries, and those of the other Sun'ozi. That is inexcusable. I am not like that, nor are the other Rex'ulti."

Ty crawled up from a nearby tide pool. "Neither are the Kisq'ali."

I whirled around, confused. I didn't expect this at all. Apologies from my enemies? "How do I know you aren't deceiving me?"

Ax began to walk closer to us. "I swear it on the life of my unborn child."

My eyes went wide.

"I don't want to raise my son or daughter in the midst of warfare," Ax continued, putting an arm around Lee'yah and a hand on her belly. "I want to be a leader for my clan that can foster community and collaboration between the other clans."

"Agreed!" Ty chimed in, grabbing Kaia next to him with his tentacles and holding her in his arms.

Sha'nah squeezed my hand. "I'll be making a home here with you, Gar'ek, because you are my mate, and I want peace for our future family." My stomach dropped. My mate wanted to have a family with me?!

I was torn. On the one hand, I wanted to avenge my father and my people. But I knew my father would also want the Sun'ozi to thrive. A life without constant worry of attack and easily accessible resources sounded like...Tingokku. And, technically, the Sun'ozi would be in power. We just wouldn't be ruling alone.

I wanted exactly what my mate wanted. A peaceful place to raise a family.

"I'm willing to talk," I said, pulling Sha'nah against my side. "As long as our mates are there too."

Ax and Ty smiled. "Deal," they said in unison, and Sha'nah reached up on her toes to kiss my cheek.

And by the gods, I think I actually blushed.

EPILOGUE

SHAWNA

ONE STAR CYCLE LATER

"WE'RE GOING TO BE LATE," I said in between giggles, as Gar'ek brought me to orgasm yet again with his dexterous vines. I'd honestly lost count of how many times I'd climaxed today.

Ever since I'd found out I was pregnant, he couldn't keep his hands, or anything else, off me. Pregnancy made my body incredibly sensitive to the softest touch, and he refused to let that go to waste.

I was thrilled, of course. But it also took ten times as long to get anything done.

I finally had to push him away and fix my furs. "*Enough*, my mate."

Go figure. Whenever I used a firm voice, it only made him want me more.

He shook his head and straightened his sepal. Jeez. Even on Co'sentyx men had it easy when it came to getting dressed.

"I am ready. Let's go!" He hurried me out the door, and we headed to the big bonfire.

We held this bonfire once every season with all the clans. It was a huge celebration with food and games and drink, a real testament to the way the clans had managed to come together as one after all this time.

Don't get me wrong, it wasn't a completely smooth transition. Definitely shaky at the start, after the leaders met to iron out the rules and then returned to their people to go over them.

Not everyone was happy, in fact some initially refused to participate. It was perhaps understandable: many of them had known nothing but constant battle for their entire lives. But as time went on and the clans began to interact more peacefully with one another, people came to at least accept it. Others were happier than ever. And the children were able to be children again.

The fire on the shore was already burning brightly, and revelers were everywhere. Some were drinking, others playing games similar to chess and cornhole. Kids ran about on the sand playing tag. It was amazing to see all the clans together.

I spied Leah and waved to her.

As we made our way over, I saw Ax'ryon's mother holding Leah's new baby girl. Her long fins dragged a bit in the sand, but she still looked so happy with little Ma'yana in her arms.

I pulled Gar'ek over to them and kissed Ax'ryon's mother on her shimmering cheek. Then I cooed over Ma'yana. She was so adorable. She had human skin and black-rimmed eyes with little orange fins running down her head and back. She would be a redhead for sure, with sweet, webbed toes.

Lee'yah hugged me. "How are you feeling?" she asked.

"Amazing," I said, looking up at Gar'ek. He winked.

"Well, you're glowing, Shawna. Pregnancy really suits you," Kaia said, walking over to me. Ty slithered up behind her and bumped a tentacle to Gar'ek's vine in greeting.

Yep. It was a whole different planet now.

I'd worried that I'd miss Earth, but with a thriving community, good friends, the most incredible mate, and a baby on the way, I didn't really miss it at all.

And I couldn't wait to find out what was in store for my newfound family.

Looking for what to read next?
Check out my books page here:
https://www.jinxlayne.com/books2
You can sign up for my newsletter via my website:
www.jinxlayne.com
It's the best way to hear about new and upcoming releases, plus get access to exclusives and bonus content.

And as always, if you liked this book please post a review on any of your preferred platforms. Reviews are the lifeblood of independent authors like me, and I welcome your opinions and feedback.
Thanks for reading!

ABOUT THE AUTHOR

Jinx Layne writes short, steamy, alien, monster, and paranormal romance - believing love transcends *all* boundaries. She enjoys traveling, especially to any place with a beach, finding waves to be the best sleeping aid. The perfect day includes coffee, a good book, and her feet up on the lanai.

Join Jinx's mailing list for new and upcoming releases (and exclusive content!) here: www.jinxlayne.com

facebook.com/jinx.layne.7

instagram.com/jinxlayne

www.ingramcontent.com/pod-product-compliance
Lightning Source LLC
Chambersburg PA
CBHW020130180626
46810CB00004B/1493